Fugue XXIX

Forrest Aguirre

RAW DOG SCREAMING PRESS

Fugue XXIX Copyright © 2005
by Forrest Aguirre

Published by Raw Dog Screaming Press
Hyattsville, MD

First Paperback Edition

Cover image: Terry Rentzepis, www.alltenthumbs.com
Book design: Jennifer C. Barnes

Printed in the United States of America

ISBN: 1-933293-12-8

Library of Congress Control Number: 2005929005

www.rawdogscreaming.com

To my wife and children for tolerating my need to scratch pen against paper. And to those who encouraged me to write and those who told me I'd never make it as a writer—I thank you both for your motivation.

Acknowledgements

A number of these stories have been previously published:

"Downstream Flow: A Fugue" - *Flesh & Blood*

"Tickets, Please" - *Crown of Bones*

"Four Canopus" - *Exquisite Corpse*

"Convergence on a Panoptic Newtonian:
    The Interstices of Heaven" - *Apocalypse Fiction*

"The Night Factory" - *Vicious Shivers*

"Bearing Seed" - *Yellow Bat Review*

"The Reverie Styx" - *Flesh & Blood*

"Loyal" - *DeathGrip*

"Precognitive Myopia" - *Strangewood Tales*

"Waiting for Felicity" - *Journal of Experimental Fiction*

"Over Alsace" - *Polyphony*

"Return from Abaddon" - *Flesh & Blood*

"In the Place Where Suffering Was Not" - *The Dream People*

"The Universal Language of Silence" - *Twilight Showcase*

"Kaleidoscopes of Africa" - *3rd Bed*

"Frenzy" - *Problem Child*

"Matriarch" - *All-Star Zeppelin Adventure Stories*

"The Butterfly Artist" - *The Butterfly Artist*

"The Nut Lady's Cabin" - *Earwig Flesh Factory*

"The Bones of Ndundi" - *Notre Dame Review*

"The Color of Laughter" - *The Fifth Dimension*

"Queen Phoebe" - *Whispers from the Shattered Forum*

"The Further Adventures of Star Boy" - *Surreal Magazine*

Table of Contents

Downstream Flow: A Fugue

Downriver a calico-clad woman, baby strapped to her back with a sunshine yellow sling, washed laundry on a flat rock as had been done for hundreds, perhaps thousands of years. She waved her prune-fingers and smiled at two handsome ebony-skinned canoe polers who offered their morning greetings and smiles in return. She wondered what sort of catch the fisherman had procured that morning then noticed a water-borne cavalcade following behind the boat; sure evidence of flooding: three vaguely human figures, all in a line, here a blonde-haired, pale-faced head, there a black arm, there a white sunburned leg, cattle horns atop human heads and two, sometimes three different faces—black and white—peeled off and superimposed on one another; a marching moil of parts and pieces caucasoid, negroid and bovine. The cadaverous caravan floated slowly along the current, following in the canoe's wake toward the colonial outpost a mile or so downstream. *Odd fish*, thought the laundry woman, *a strange catch.*

The carrion parade first reached the shantytown just outside the wooden walls of the outpost proper. Thin-ribbed, hollow-eyed children swarmed out of aluminum-roofed huts and into the river, expending their death throes in a final effort to glean sustenance from the bounty of the floods. Most earned a good thumping with a canoe pole, some drowned, while a group of five boys wrested a cattle torso from the stream, ripping into the bloated guts and filling their voracious holes at the water's edge as the procession passed the edge of town and entered the poorer parts of the colonial quarter. Upriver, cannibals and crocodiles sat sated on the banks, enjoying the afterglow of the levy they had charged on the passing fishermen earlier that morning.

Cibembe, slender whore and town gossip, was first within the fortressed walls to purchase the fishermen's wares. She pointed at a white head, grinning with satisfaction as she threw her colonial ducats into the dugout: "Ah, those ears, those huge white ears! With those I will hear every bit of rumor that leaves the white man's mouth. I will know when the police come, where the best parties are, who is the best-paying client. The secrets of Ngome will be mine." She entered the water, knife in hand, to retrieve the ears. Upstream, five children lay dying on the riverbanks, their poisoned stomachs collapsing in on themselves as they crawled away from a hollow set of cow ribs.

Nigel Dawson, Esquire, exited a hut three doors down from the harlot. He quickly zipped his trousers, tossing some coin to his favorite "mistress," then ran out to pick his choice from the flowing meat wagon. Bright and pink, protruding from a charcoal head, swayed a tongue. Three crowns and a ducat later the tongue was his. Now he would speak convincingly before both tribal councils and colonial courts, something no white lawyer had been able to do until now. His renown and his wealth would spread like wildfire. Upstream a woman turned deaf, whispers of official atrocities and backroom brokering echoing in her mind.

A circus had entered town a few nights before. There, under a brilliant red and yellow canopy, Giardino, the midget, dreamed of being tall, unafraid, towering over all others. The splashing of water broke his reverie and he woke, approaching the liquid pronouncement. Three ducats—his life's savings—went into a pair of long, slender black legs, like those of a giant cricket. Seven feet tall he stood now, towering head and shoulders above autochthon and invader alike. Upstream a lawyer fell under the clubs of a council of grizzled elders—"no white man should speak like a black," they said. "Such a line should not be crossed.

Besides, we must protect ourselves. If the authorities got wind of such improprieties, retribution fall on us and him alike!"

Venefatt, the clown, shopped for a happy face. He found one two layers down in a pile of stripped skin—a smiling visage, just the right size and shape. He threw in his pay then affixed the cheery mask to his own dour portrait. It fit perfectly. Now he would make the children laugh rather than run, smile rather than cry. Upstream an erstwhile midget collapsed as the sickly thinness of his newly-acquired legs filtered up through his trunk, arms and face, sinking his cheeks and distending his belly. His eyes fell out of hollow sockets onto the ochre earth six feet, seven inches below.

At the end of the line of brightly colored tents, Cincoglio, the ringmaster, smiled greedily as he purchased a pair of cattle horns. He would affix them to his sideshow mermaid, making her irresistible song all the more terrifying, her sewn-up lips all the more necessary for safety. *Audiences will gladly pay more*, he thought, *for the privilege of seeing my monster*. Upstream a black-faced clown was being arrested for performing without a license and for providing a false identification card—obviously stolen. The penalty for natives impersonating colonists was stiff—stiff as a rhinoceros hide whip. This black clown would pay the penalty.

Geld Vansina, the rubber plantation owner, opened his purse and waded out to intercept the passing boat. After some haggling, he threw two crowns to the boatmen and took his share—two humungous black hands to be used as a warning to plantation employees of what happens to thieves: an eye for an eye, a hand for a bucket of stolen rubber. Upstream a siren popped her sutures with the end of a sharp bullhorn and sang the ringmaster's last lullaby.

At the deep end of the river, where the channel spills into a great lake, Arthur Stokes waited in his rowboat as those of his métier, yet not of his race, passed close by. He threw them a ducat for his needs—a white head. *Excellent*, he thought as he took the proffered melon, *I don't have to take the ears off—one less step.* He dropped the head directly into the grinder. Upriver a plantation owner tugged at his throat, trying to remove the immense hands that had somehow remembered their past and become vengeful. Stokes, however, did not heed the screams coming from within the fortress walls. He steered his boat out into the open water, happy to have fresh chum with which to bait fish. On the shoreline a woman with a baby slung on her back washed laundry as had been done for hundreds, perhaps thousands, of years.

The Mystic Flower

"Thou whose mouth is a flame
With its seven-edged sword proceeding,
Come! I am writhing with despair
Like a snake taken in a snare,
Moaning thy mystical name
Till my tongue is torn and bleeding!"

"Ave Adonai"
Aleister Crowley

The Mystic Flower glooms above you, Cheshire white smile gleaming an alertness entirely absent from its single droop-lidded, drowsy cycloptic eye. Nevertheless, the eye sparkles sunrays in a beam panoptic, incinerating uncertainty and despair, illuminating the mind of the faithful, replacing the void blackness with hope, a shining ray of joy. This light casts a faint reflective glow on each of The Mystic Flower's seven petals.

Hunter Green

What would the English do without their eccentrics? I cannot imagine. The sun might as well not shine, as English society not squeeze out strangeness from its interstices. Culture would cease at once, for what else might the social order compare itself against, but the contradiction in its midst? One wonders, before the advent of the daily newspapers, how England survived at all as a cultural entity, with only the village idiot or local town drunkard as a foil against which the body compared itself.

Thankfully, in this publication, you hold in your hands the very cement of our good society. And no one provides a better catalyst, a better example of social irresponsibility, than the self appointed "Magi," Ogden Covent. For in Ogden Covent we find an antithesis against which the success of English society, in its capacity to establish good judgment and order, may be measured.

Mr. Covent, on first glance, seemed rather harmless, if a bit odd, in his charcoal-grey highland kilt and black top hat. Only on closer examination did his apparel betray more than just an anachronistic taste. The sporran that hung on the front of his kilt was carved of ivory in the form of two skulls, in profile, kissing one another. The orbitals were filled with gold eyeballs, inlaid with amethyst irises, which rolled in their sockets. From his neck hung a silver pentagram, while his ears were both pierced through with enough golden hoops to satisfy a boatload of pirates. A dandy indeed! But a dandy given to grotesquery.

Our conversation lasted the course of an afternoon, during which time Covent showed me around his not-insubstantial estate. The grounds were overgrown, the main complex dilapidated, though not shoddy in its initial construction—just very, very old and un-cared for. Certain windows were cracked, shingles were missing from the roof, and the water from the well pump was brackish. It is rumored that a visitor to the estate died after drinking the water of this well.

Yet, despite the imperfections of the buildings and grounds, the estate held a rustic charm—quite like Covent himself. His eyelids appeared ever-weary, half-closed at all times, but they hid a certain clarity in the eyes themselves—a knowing-ness that affected me powerfully. As it must be with his followers, I yearned to know what he knew and to understand the energy in his eyes. Only the ridiculousness of his missing teeth—gapped as badly as the surrounding picket fence, and his balding head—sparse as the thatching on the un-used stable's roof, kept me from being mesmerized by his soothing voice and calm demeanor.

It was not difficult to understand, upon meeting some of his followers, how he held sway over the cultists. Most were young, all of them gangly, as if under-nourished, and each had about him or her (most of them were women) a great lack of self-confidence, evinced by their turning to him for approval to answer any of my questions. A demure expression of downcast eyes fell on those whom I questioned until, after a non-verbal interchange of glances and nods between the acolytes and their master, their eyes brightened, as if they now had Covent's permission to speak, albeit not as freely as I would have preferred.

What little I did learn from his congregation might not, I am afraid, shed any new light on the inner workings of the cult, but the interviewees' mannerisms spoke volumes about the group's interface with the outside world. Slow, halting sentences, the aversion of the eyes at critical moments (always away from me and toward Covent), and roundabout answers belied at least some fear that bad things might befall those who gave the "wrong" answers. Distractions were frequent, but more on this later.

Though an underlying unease could be detected at almost all times, this fear subsided when the disciples expressed admiration for their teacher. All of them seemed genuinely grateful and gave thanks that Mr. Covent, through his mystical teachings, had given them direction and some hope in life. They claimed to have come to clarity—most of them were opium addicts, alcoholics, prostitutes, or victims of severe abuse before their association with Covent—from his clear explanation of the working cosmos and their place therein.

Covent's universal paradigm is a strange syncretic mélange containing elements of secular hedonism, Rosicrucianism, eastern religions, Kabbalism, pagan ritual, and the lowest debaucheries of the Knights

Templar. Despite these fragments, though, the central tenant of Covent's belief system rests on what he calls "The Recognition of the Sublime." He defines the sublime as that which inspires awe and both its guises of reverence and of fear. Intensity of experience and the deepest emotions, whether "good" or "bad," he claims, create a sacred space in which worshippers communicate with the universe on a level of raw understanding, inexpressible in any language. These experiences can, indeed ought, to be focused and concentrated through "art"—a euphemism for the enjoyment of a number of activities including, but not limited to, drug consumption, magic ritual, sexual promiscuity, and, yes, the enjoyment of the arts (as defined by mainstream English society), whether in the creative aspect, or as the entertained.

This "Recognition of the Sublime" proved a most annoying precept during my interviews, as it provided Covent and his followers a convenient dodge to my questions. From time to time—and at the most inopportune moments—Covent or a follower would fall silent in mid-sentence, stare off into the distance at something that had caught his or her eye, then begin ululating very loudly at a beautiful object, a flash of sunlight, or, seemingly, nothing at all—at least nothing that I could perceive. I learned, between the many interruptions, that these noises, which sounded for all the world like the cries of Mohammedan women at a funeral, were a verbal expression of the spiritual energy that one (one trained to recognize it, that is) experiences in the presence of the sublime. One can only imagine that their rituals rival the markets of Marrakesh for sheer noise. It is a wonder, given the volume of their cries, that the cult's secret rituals remain secret at all.

I felt, at times, that these vocal ecstasies were used as a way of avoiding my admittedly uncomfortable questions regarding the group's finances, the follower's lives before their conversion, and the influence that Covent held over them. I left with more questions than I had when

I first arrived. Nevertheless, I view my interviews not as a series of failures, but as a segue into further research—and an affirmation that if, as some believe, England is defined by its variance from its most extreme elements, our home land will be secure in law and clear judgment for some time to come.

James Bangerter
Looking Glass Chronicle
July, 1897

Cerulean

A strange tea garden grew up from the lawn outside Mrs. Sarah Scripp's drawing room. Out of the ground grew wicker chairs, all in a circle, surmounted by frills, velvet ribbons, lace, dresses billowing up in a bouquet of fabric, topped by flowered sun hats nodding, turning to one another. A dozen or more pale faces spoke from between the flowers and the fabric. Snippets of conversation wafted up from the garden like pollen carried aloft on a spring breeze.

"Perhaps the unfortunate passing of her parents has caught up with her."

A chorus of "Mmmm."

"Dreadful, those coolies."

"Ah, but convenient."

"And cheap!"

"Only if handled properly, as her parents found out."

A short, respectful silence.

"One wonders, though, if her husband is to blame."

"Likely, he is. He's not good stock, that one."

"A *parvenu*, no doubt about it."

"But he never seems to have treated her ill."

"Not in public, my dear."

"Remember, the money was hers."

"Yes, he bought up. A merchant's son, correct?"

"Correct. Cotton, but not overly successful."

"One wonders why she would keep all the money for herself."

"No, but she did not! She tithed it to that Covent creature."

"Tithed? She gave it all!"

"And that's not all she gave."

Groans and giggles.

"Still, some sympathy for the poor girl. She was taken in by the newsies about Covent."

"Bothersome journalists. Ah, no offence, Mrs. Frist."

"None taken, my dear."

"But she never would have been mesmerized by Covent, had her husband not been reading the newsies."

"I have forbidden my Georgie from taking the newspaper."

"Quite."

Lavender

April, 1898

Spring has finally finished her crawl out from under a deep, cold winter. It seems that Hades had fed Persephone some particularly large pomegranate seeds this autumn past, at least in these isles. Demeter has seen fit to celebrate the return of her daughter by afflicting me with hay fever. She always has been capricious that way.

My mother, unlike Persephone, will not be returning home. Doctor

Fulsom tells us—father and I—that Mum is not well, but that there is nothing he can do—legally—to restrain her. He blames what he calls the "new legislation," though it is more than ten years old.

She has been gone, in all, two months now. Father would divorce her, as is his right, if the allegations of adultery are, indeed, true. But he dares not, as Mum's money would fall to her and, hence, to me. I think, for this, he hates me.

After the doctor left us, my father discarded honor in favor of rum and gin, drinking to excess, smashing the sitting room, and causing a great din. His wrath since has been nigh uncontrollable, and I question whether even Grandmum's move (father's mum, of course) into our home will quell his anger.

A few weeks ago I went to school with a bruised eye—the result of father's drunken outlash, though this was not the first time he had behaved badly at home, only the first time that I, or my Mum, for that matter, had a mark to show for his temper. After determining, among themselves, the source of my injury, my erstwhile friends were careful to avoid me, as if I were cursed, or might sprout horns and cloven feet at any moment—the evil progeny of equally evil parents. Perhaps they think that I am paying for Mum's alleged sins.

This begs the further question of *That Man's* disposition. Did he entrance my mother, or free her from an abusive husband? Is he, as some suppose, a modern Hades? Or is he a masculine Demeter?

And I wonder if Persephone's friends abandoned her after her curse? At least she had a *mother*.

Crimson

Resurrecting Ophelia

Overview: "Resurrecting Ophelia" is a cleansing ritual whose name refers to the Ophelia character of Shakespeare's *Hamlet*, whose indecision and lack of self-motivation ultimately prove her demise. This is a preliminary ritual in preparation for "Sophia's Marriage," as performed by Magi Ogden Covent (cf vol. XII—*Meditative Sacraments*). The initiate participant, acting as Ophelia, symbolically dies and is then resurrected anew, sure of herself, resolved to live as a self-existent being, free from the bonds of indecision and over-reliance on others.

The Ritual: The initiate dons a dress of English Renaissance style (the three known to be used by Covent's several brides were not only of this style, but of this provenience as well) and is then bedecked with necklaces, bracelets, anklets, and tiaras woven of columbine, fennel, rue, daisies, crow-flowers, nettles and "long purples." The party then proceeds to a slow-flowing river as the initiate chants:

> And will he not come again?
> And will he not come again?
> No, no, he is dead;
> Go to thy death bed,
> He will never come again.

The initiate, still chanting, wades into the water, followed by nine of her companions, all dressed in ancient Greek clothing (to represent The Muses). They lower the proxy Ophelia into the water as they chant:

> Hey non nonny nonny
> Hey nonny nonny.

They submerge the initiate while chanting, then let her float to the surface. This is repeated nine times. The Magi, also dressed in ancient Greek robes, and riding a donkey (symbolizing, of course, Dionysus/Bacchus), cries out:

> Is she to be buried
> in Christian burial
> that willfully seeks her own salvation?

To which the initiate responds:

> You must sing a-down a-down.

The culmination of the ritual commences with the Magi's call of:

> Too much water hast thou,
> poor Ophelia!

Upon which the Muses carry Ophelia out of the river. The Magi then explains to the initiate that these nine Muses are the Maenads who, before their subjugation to Apollo, wrought mischief on all who fell into their disfavor. Then, dismounting from the donkey and casting off his robes, he, naked, declares:

> I am the sun god!
> Only in subjection to me
> may your gift of new life
> remain complete!

The "Sophia's Marriage" ritual follows immediately thereafter.

From *Encyclopedia of Magicks: Contemporary Ritual, vol IV*, Randall Amundsen, ed., pp. 312-23.

Fugue XXIX

Orange

Precision was built into the architecture at Doctor Elmund Lawson's office, from the crisply-etched frosted glass window advertising "Lawson Medical Practices" to the finely-fluted neo-gothic archway over the front door, to the exquisite bronze lion's head door handle. Passers-by were seemingly compelled by an unseen, but clearly-sensed, air of propriety to hold their heads a bit higher, even the lowest street urchin assuming an aristocratic mien that Dr. Lawson hoped would serve as a prophylactic against debilitation and disease.

He held little hope, though, for the crone now bowing at his door. Her smile was wide, her teeth a decaying picket fence. And, though one eye held a certain blue spark, its brilliance was almost completely shrouded by the folds of skin that hooded over it. A milky glass eye in the other socket drew attention away from the one spot of beauty on the old hag. She was wrapped against the February cold by grey scarves that released an ancient stench as she removed them on entering the doctor's office.

"Good day," her voice scratched out through a smile as she bowed again, lifting her hat only briefly to reveal balding greyness.

"And to you," the doctor stated with a flat voice as he pulled his portly frame out of the high leather chair in which he sat. He stood, with much effort, then stared at the old lady as if studying a curious, but previously un-catalogued, disease. After a long, uncomfortable silence in which the older woman merely smiled and nodded, the doctor assumed a business-like tone.

"I presume you have the paperwork, Ms. Burke?"

"Aye, 'tis here," she reached into some hidden pocket and extracted a slim stack of documents. She placed them on the table, then stepped back from the desk as Lawson cautiously retrieved the papers, never taking his eyes off the woman.

"I am an organized midwife," she said with pastiched haughtiness, tilting her head and pursing her lips.

He donned a pair of spectacles, then perused the paperwork, looking up from time to time to snatch a glimpse of the old woman. After a round of grunts and "Hmm," he set the papers down, sat on the corner of his desk, and removed his glasses.

"Your report indicates that the child is well. How is my client?"

"She rests from her labors. Doubt that in Earth is fire, doubt that the stars do move, doubt truth to be a liar, but do not doubt my master's love, to the beautiful Ophelia. As for Azaziah: the King, his son's alive."

"Azaziah," the doctor looked at the woman with an expression of disdain approaching disgust. "How long did the labor last?"

"From the ascendance of Orion to that time when yonder star that's westward from the pole, had made his course to illumine that part of heaven. Where now it burns, the bell then tolling one."

Lawson sighed, shook his head.

"I'm going to regret asking this, but what is your assessment of the child?"

"Praise Pan, for the woman's womb hath brought forth a son, virile and full of power and warmth. I very well agree with you, in the hopes of him: it is a gallant child; one, that (indeed) physics the subject, makes old hearts fresh: they that went on crutches ere he was borne, desire yet their life, to see him a man," the old woman coughed, then continued in a hoarse voice. "He is the one that the Magi prophesied would come to redeem us from the oppression of dull vision. Through him, our eyes will be open, and we shall have knowledge."

"Ah, very good. And the baby's mother?"

"A joyful mother of one goodly son. Yet is his mother fair. And this woman is now become a goddess."

"I will report to her husband that she has survived the ordeal."

23

"I grant that she is a woman, but withal a woman that the Magi took to wife!" The old woman's voice raised in pitch and intensity, her expression twisted in anger.

The doctor turned red in the face then, with carefully-measured restraint that barely concealed the rage that had suddenly risen in him, dismissed her: "Madame, I bid you good day!"

The old midwife left, and the aura of precision and decorum that had been banished by her presence, soon re-entered the room. Lawson held his head up high as the sun began to spill light in through the windows, casting sharp shadows from its perfect sill.

Cyan

Men, brethren, gods, goddesses, sisters. I am honored to stand among you who have devoted yourselves to the realization of the sublime. Several times our critics have issued forth false prophecy foretelling our community's demise. We were a passing fad, a ludicrous fancy that would disperse within a year. But we remained. "Two years and their collapse is imminent! Three and they will be extinct! Four, they will be but a memory!" they bellowed from their foul throats. Yet we remain. Persecutions have raged against us, even so much that there are martyrs from our congregation who, even now, labor as angels of light in preparation for the coming revelation. It is this coming revelation that compels me to speak to you at this hour.

Twenty years ago today I sat brooding, one morning, over the mechanization of man. It was a pleasant day among the green hills of Sussex. The sun shone brilliantly across a field of daisies outside my window. The air was fragrant with grass and freshly fallen rain. A trio of falcons soared overhead, scouring the valleys for prey.

But despite this beautiful scene, a dimness clouded my mind. In the hills beyond my window, lay several country manors, which were host to some of the most beautiful gardens in the region. Lilies and Delphiniums dotted the flats in perfectly concentric circles, lemon trees were lined up like yellow polka-dotted soldiers on parade, Lavender grew unchecked by any natural opponents—enemies were swiftly weeded out by fastidious gardeners who raged at the sight of a mis-placed weed. Nature was hostage to man, I thought, as man was becoming hostage to machine.

My contemplations were confirmed when I took a walk through the countryside. Not far from my flat was a stately mansion that bespoke the quisessentialism of being English. Two crowned lions rampant guarded the wrought-iron gate, and at their statued feet, on either side of the gate, a bright yellow pot of flowers. Spreading out along the brick walls that braced the lions was a culled and cropped hedgerow—a first defense against intruders. I reflected on the two types of plants: the flowers, Voss's Laburnum, and the hedges, Oval Leaf Privet, are both toxic to man. Strange, I thought, that we have wrought nature to keep nature out.

I continued on, my thoughts filled with hedges and fences, un-naturally organized flower gardens being fed by man-made canals where water was never meant to run. I was about to succumb in body and spirit to this neo-classical nightmare when I spotted an irregularity in the landscape. I cut across a farmer's field towards the visual scar near the horizon, irreverently fighting my way through trimmed hedges, intentionally treading a zig-zag trail over the neat rows of grain.

I broke through the opposite hedge and stumbled into a revelation, an epiphanic moment, some might say, a vision. I was enclosed in the womb of the woods and before me squatted the half-ruined skeleton of a seemingly ancient stone and thatch house. The structure had been gutted by fire some time ago, and the charred remains of one wall had sloughed off into what was quickly becoming an overgrown garden. The once-domesticated flowers had burst their boundaries and were joined by their wilder cousins, though I failed to understand how this pictur-esque scene could have emerged from the ground with such a dearth of sunlight. In spite of my questions, I gloried in each sapling and every noxious weed that sprouted up through man's handiwork. Nature had retaken the lead, slowly purging itself of impurity.

I must have remained in that dark grove for some time. Hunger finally compelled me to exit the woods, but as I breached the forest wall, I noticed that evening was falling. But not only was the sun descending, a low line of fierce, dark clouds swept in from the southeast, driven by a cold wind. I could see sheets of rain and bolts of lightning erupting from the bottom of the clouds, creating a bow-wake of destruction as the storm lumbered from hill to hill. Transfixed by the immensity and ferocity of the oncoming storm, I could do naught but stand rooted to the earth and watch as maelstrom consumed the evening sun.

Immediately ahead of the storm blew a horizon-wide halo of leaves, tiny green ephemera against the sky, tumbling, fluttering at me like a flock of chlorophyllic birds. At that moment of perception when the stark realization of my precarious position in the path of the storm combined with the awestruck hypnosis that held my vision bound to that slow-flying green magic carpet, it was then, my brothers and sisters, that I first experienced the power of the sublime.

So complete was my transfixion that, only after the storm blew me on my back, did I realize just how fragile the human frame can be. For, despite my high-flying spirits, my body could not move quickly enough to avoid the lightning stroke that felled me like a stricken tree.

I awoke the next morning, alive, but obviously and permanently damaged by my encounter with nature's wrath. Even now some people note my slight limp—the result, of course, of electricity exiting near my ankle—and I am called, by some, The Limping Prophet. Nevertheless, I rose and walked back toward my flat—the first steps along the journey that has led me here, before you now.

My search for the sublime took many long years. I studied in Tibet, in the monasteries of Ireland. I even braved the jungles of Africa in search of the sublime. I exercised my mind, as well as my feet, exploring the ancient texts of the wise, probing the depths of the mystics in order to try to satisfy my insatiable appetite for the sublime. This hunger drove me, a spiritual vagabond, ever onward, staying a short while in one place, then moving on to the next. But it seemed that no matter how much I feasted on the mysteries of the beyond, I remained famished.

I settled, for a time, in Ravello, Italy, along the Amalfi coast, there studying the ancient rites of Dionysus, or Bacchus, the Greco-Roman god of wine. I had read about the practice, in that city, of those partaking the sacraments whispering "Bacchus" after the holy wafer had passed their lips, and wished to investigate further the rumor, as my studies to that point had led to an interest in the so-called Ecstasy Cults of the ancient Greeks and Romans.

I shall not deign to reveal all that I learned there, the many rites I saw and, yes, in which I participated. These matters are sacred to the modern Bacchanalian cult, and I wish to respect that sacred trust that was placed in me as an acolyte of the cult. But I did find, in our nighttime revelries, in The Bull Dance, and The Consumption of Bacchus, the portal to a state of being that brought on the feeling that had washed over me when I had entered that Sussex grove years before. Still, though I entered that realm of feeling that I call the picturesque, the sublime eluded me.

I left Ravello for a few days to do research at a monastery in the country. After my little foray into the dusty archives of the monastery's basement, I headed back to Ravello where I hoped to peruse the documents I had procured.

In the country near Ravello stands a grove of trees, and in that grove the ruins of a Roman temple. How old, I don't know, since Ravello was only founded in the 400's AD by Romans fleeing the gothic invasion from the north. Nevertheless, the condition of those ruins bespoke obvious antiquity. The marble columns and floor of the building were all that remained of what once must have been a bright-white beacon shining through the poplars on that rural hilltop.

The locals knew those ruins, and when I was introduced to the ancient sacramental rites, I was taken there and told the history of the site.

Beneath the hill, I was told, was once a cavern, a burial cavern dedicated to Tuchulcha, the Etruscan demoness of the underworld. Roman records indicate that carvings and statuary from well before the Etruscan period hint that this place was once a burial "womb" for worshippers of the ancient Earth-mother goddess, which had spread from Eastern Europe down the peninsula long before written records were kept. We might never have known, since the cavern was filled in by zealous Roman priests who, after burying the cavern in dirt and rock, built a temple to Mars, god of war, during the period of Roman ascension and colonization in those parts of Italy. These Mars cultists were, in turn, killed by an advance group of Goths who had penetrated deep to the south along the Amalfi coast just before the main body of Goths sacked Rome. Of course, thousands fled from before the Germanic hordes, and among these were the first settlers of Ravello, the core of which was a group of Bacchanalian acolytes who had been secretly worshipping in Rome for time untold. The pre-existence of a temple (albeit one in bad repair) and the relatively isolated location of the future city-site, attracted these followers whose religion had had to operate "underground" for a number of centuries. As you can see, my brothers and sisters, this was a place of great spiritual power, a crossroads of deific energy.

I passed this grove on my way back to Ravello and was astonished to see the high columns, between which I had whirled with my fellow worshippers, dashed to the ground. The pillars lay embedded deep in the earth where they had penetrated the temple floor and thrust through some old tombs that the Mars priests had missed in their desecration. Stooping over the newly-exposed graves, I peered in to see the walls lined with charcoal drawings, in a crude style, of bulls and men, and men with bull's heads, dancing under a ring of trees. There were also several small statues, all but one mangled or destroyed completely. I kept the last complete artifact, a small statuette of a mother-goddess giving birth to a bull-calf. This statuette now stands in our orchard outside.

Upon returning to town, I sought out an acquaintance of mine—a fellow-worshipper and locally-famous painter noted for richly-colored landscapes that entirely contradicted the bland earth-tone sensibility so prevalent in our own national galleries at the time. I found Antonio, as I shall call him, in his studio, staring at a drying canvas from his stool.

Never before had I seen him in such torpor, his glassy eyes reflecting his just-finished painting. I scanned the canvas for any clue as to his state, not wanting to startle him. Soon I, too, stood staring, an empty shell of a man before that thing that I had so earnestly been seeking—for in that painting was the sublime made manifest.

The painting shone with Antonio's customary striking palette. A thin, but intense orange line beamed along the Amalfi horizon as the rising sun lifted the inky indigo night into the sky. Stars shone high above, not as pinpoints, but as blurs, for the ground was quaking in this scene, and the pillars of the ruin I had just visited swayed and crumbled, arcing toward the ancient temple floor beneath. The trees shook, their leaves a blue-green smear on the evening sky. All seemed a-muddle, except for the foreground figures. There I saw, in clear focus, the faces and naked bodies of my fellow-worshippers, caught in that exact moment of realization that their doom was at hand. Their faces strained and bodies tensed as if their screams exited from their very pores. This clarity of emotion made me numb, chills spread over me, and that feeling that I had experienced so many years ago in the whirlwind and lightning flushed through me once again.

As many of you know, I paid Antonio to travel with me for some months after, commissioning him to find and capture the images of those whose faces most fully expressed The Realization of the Sublime, along with the attendant circumstances that evoked such emotion. Many of those paintings are displayed throughout the manor. During those months I developed my Theories of Art and Magick, in which I revealed the connection between the arts, ritual, and the sublime. You are familiar with these writings. After reading them you joined me, my brothers and sisters, in my—our—ongoing quest, and here we stand, in spite of all our critics.

Now I have taken her, and she has born me a man-child, as had been prophesied. And this man-child shall grow in stature and favor before you. As I have led you from the beautiful to the picturesque, and from the picturesque to the sublime, so shall he lead you beyond to the full realization of the sublime: The apocalyptic, which now waits for us, the consummation of all things, the ultimate flowering of the sublime. He shall lead us, my brothers and sisters, into paradise!

Address given by Ogden Covent, October 16, 1900.

Indigo

This final account, which comes to us secondhand from the nephew of Jonathan Blacksdale, one of Covent's closest followers, who was present at the hotel when Covent and his son entered the room, is the most interesting of these many stories surrounding the death of the Magi. In this final account, Blacksdale reported that Covent's wife was, indeed, among those present, thus contradicting the "official" account, but agreeing with the sworn testimony of at least three other witnesses who were cross-examined at Covent's trial:

> She was there to see her son off to becoming a man. The boy
> was, she had said, her only love-child. But, she knew, he must
> assume his role ushering in the new apocalypse. Thus, with
> tears, she let him go for the greater good of all mankind.

Why Blacksdale was never called as a witness is unknown. Perhaps Fred
Folkens, the group's lawyer, felt that to have the old man testify would
jeopardize his position vis-à-vis the judge and the public. Blacksdale's
account of what happened, as related by his nephew, might cause any
man to doubt the witness's credulity:

> Uncle Jon quoted Covent as saying that no one should,
> under any circumstances, enter the room. To do so, he
> warned, would upset the careful magical protections that he
> would soon prepare, thus endangering the efficacy of the
> rituals that would bring in the new apocalypse, the new
> paradise. "No matter how much I beg, plead, or cry for help,
> you must not do it. You will not enter this room, only after I
> have exited. Is this clear?"

Covent and the boy entered the empty room with naught but a dagger,
some candles, and several sticks of chalk. Both were dressed in ceremo-
nial garb: purple robes and fanciful headdresses in the old tricorn form,
emblazoned with stitched yellow magical sigils. The door was closed,
and for several hours the only sounds that issued from the room were
Covent's basso and the pre-pubescent boy's soprano chantings, along
with the sounds of chalk being scratched along the walls and floor.

> But then—and here Uncle Jon would speak more slowly,
> very careful about the words he chose—then, he said, there
> were other voices chanting, other feet plodding around in

that room, other scratchings along the floor and walls. "Oh, we wanted to peek in," he told me, "the sublime was upon us, no doubt about that! But we wanted so badly to witness the ushering in of the apocalyptic. We all looked at each other, wanting so badly to see, to know. But we obeyed the command. Only Covent's wife succumbed to temptation, as one of her high standing must be sorely tempted, above that which an ordinary man or woman could bear. She reached for the door, but our gazes fell upon her and she withdrew her hand, as if stung by a wasp. A power was upon us all."

This chanting continued for some time, but eventually the boy's voice faded among the din, while Covent's voice grew louder and more urgent. Blacksdale claims that even more voices joined the throng, as if the room was filled with people:

"And when we expected the room to burst open with people or spirits or demons or whatever was in that place, the Magi screamed. It was pure, frantic terror, unrestrained by reason. There were scuffling sounds and bangs, as of a fight taking place, then complete silence."

The group, obedient to their leader's command, kept the door shut, though many would later claim that among Covent's screams were pleas for help and pity. Only after an hour of this haunting silence—it was well into the night at this point—did she open the door. The rest of the account is in line with all the others:

"We opened the door and entered the room. A few of the candles were still burning, but most of the light therein came from the waxing moon, as it came through the open windows. The walls and floor were covered in symbols, diagrams, and writing, all in the several languages that Covent had studied over the course of his searches: Sanskrit, Hebrew, Egyptian, Farsi, Korean, Tibetan. Mingled among it all were sketches of tumultuous landscapes and natural disasters. Earthquakes, hurricanes, volcanoes, fire, and floods were all portrayed in a delicate, though unfinished manner. We were mesmerized by this because, while all of us were cognizant of Covent's views on the sacredness of art, none of us had either seen him create, nor seen his artistic creations. Perhaps he was saving all his creativity for this last ritual. While most of us were busy marveling at this work, she was crumpled on her knees, sobbing. Before her sat her son, cross-legged, in the middle of a thaumaturgic circle. He looked immaculate, so noble, sitting there unmoving, eyes closed in meditation. It did not take long, though, to realize that the pallor of his skin was not caused by the moonlight, but, rather, that though the boy sat upright, he was quite cold and dead. As we stared, a bee crawled forth from within the boy's robes, near the neck, as if it were transporting pollen from out of the petals of a bloom. The bee took flight and exited through one of the windows. It took a moment to find Covent, who was curled up in a fetal position in the darkest corner of the room. All the chalk-drawn symbols and images around him were smudged and smeared. His clothes lay in tattered ribbons all around him, and the dagger which he had taken into the room with him never was found, either on or off the property."

The missing dagger mentioned by Blacksdale was cited as evidence-by-absence that Covent killed the boy—not necessarily with the dagger—and threw away the instrument to absolve himself of guilt, a modern

MacBeth, as the prosecution put it. This was thought by the judge who tried the case, to be enough to send Covent to the gallows, despite his maniacal disposition—medical records indicate that, by this time, Covent had plumbed the depths of insanity. Nevertheless, the court records indicate that Covent was:

> ...guilty of manslaughter, and is thus sentenced to be hanged in three day's time. Since Mr. Covent's will designates his deceased son as sole inheritor, Covent's estate and properties shall be forfeit to the royal government.

From *The Many Demises of Ogden Covent*, by Arthur Phillingrad.

The Mystic Flower is fallen, is fallen. You see its eye still half-open, but there is no life within. Petals blanche white and the stem withers ashes-to-ashes. Then: A spark of resurrecting life? But no, the lid curls black from flame within as the pupil jets fire, consuming itself in self-conflagration. And he is no one, twitching there. And you are no one. Your womb-fruit decimated in the drought that was your ever-searching life, your fortune squandered. And you are left without even a name.

Tickets, Please

He wakes sitting, face pressed against the soot-stained glass as the wheels clackity clack over iron rail. It smells like a charnel house. He smudges the window muck with a sleeve and stares out at the smoky gray sky—sullied mists rise, polluting the air over an immense plain textured by cavernous cracks that glow of magma.

The passenger turns and startles at the corpse seated next to him. It is Misses Easton, the widow from down the street, known for killing her neighbor's pets and putting razors in children's apples—not everyone thinks her husband's death accidental. Now she has joined him among the dead.

Other bodies fill the car: Captain Grody, the bigoted police chief who killed several blacks "in self defense"; Father Sullivan, who spread The Word with almost the same vigor as he spread altar boys' legs; the gossip Mary Felixton, notorious for spreading the lie that Jake McGrew molested children when it was she who had violated her niece. Twenty others sat decaying in the car, some mummified and desiccated, others bloated with putrescence, some with eyes agape, others eyes closed, others with void sockets.

He stands, scoots to the aisle, careful not to upset the dead, wondering why he is not among them. He walks to the front of the car, desperate to leave the rotting remains of those he knew and despised in life. A flick of the door's lever and he passes from the coach to the engine, briefly inhaling the sweet-rotting air in between.

Heat bleeds from the engine's walls, pistons deafening as he yells to converse with the engineer. No response. He recognizes the tattooed arms of Joe Bender, knuckles bruised from battering his wife, son's blood caked underneath his fingernails. The passenger turns back, noticing the rump end of the whore Kathleen DiMattio protruding from the blazing coal furnace. Her skeleton smiles between charred lips, the same gleaming grin that ruined a hundred families.

As he returns to the passenger car, a loud "SNAP!" echoes out as the arms of the dead raise high above their heads, holding tickets aloft as if waiting for him to inspect them. He tentatively reaches out to grasp the nearest sigil-laden pass, then stops, a strap-razor in his hand preventing him from taking the proffered slips. He lowers the razor and laughs out loud, for now he remembers—he is the conductor. He smiles and takes the tickets. The corpses smile back, leering in graveyard corruption over all their slit throats.

Four Canopus

Fatimah watched the organs fly from their body cavity as his automobile disintegrated in a spray of fiberglass and through-bolts. Accidents in Cairo are seldom tidy. As his eyes faded dead, he saw one last glimpse: Osiris, God of the Underworld, catching the organs in canopic jars to be weighed against Fatimah's soul, thus determining the dictates of eternal justice. Allah would not be pleased that a mere idol had intercepted one of the faithful—well, parts of the faithful—before he had reached paradise.

These were the contents of the jars:

IMSETY: A liver—pickled in cheap wine and thin beer. Soft and cracked through with rivulets of burning alcohol. A deep brown topographical map, complete with ragged peaks and clear flowing *wadis*. An overtaxed sack shot full of holes.

QUEBEHSENUF: A heart (Professional Egyptologists will note here a contradiction—Fatimah's intestines were unavailable at the moment of Osiris' catch, thus, in His eagerness, He grabbed the nearest available organ)—Incarnadine from toughness, not blood flow. More ruby mineral than muscle, yet ruby flawed. A tough, brittle thing. Pockmarked and bruised from self-abuse. Blood coursed through it like cold water through a cavern—the housing stiff and unmoving, cored out by a bitter liquid until the structure collapses in on itself.

HAPY: Lungs—Scarred with black furrows carved by opium smoke. Wheezy pouches frayed from yelling at wife and child. Depositories of toxic odors gathered through unethical business practice. Bellows of grime. Cilia stilled by tar and nicotine.

Fugue XXIX

DUAMUTIF: A stomach—Stretched to excess. Flaccid with gluttonous over-stuffing. An acid-churning well of worry and guilt, deception made manifest in indigestion. A treasure chest of lipids, sugar and vinegar. Clearing house of burning bile vomit—much to the joy of the liver, which quivered in fear beneath whenever the stomach was filled. A bucket of filth, unclean contents hiding from Koranic law.

Perhaps Allah wouldn't mind Osiris' interference after all.

Convergence on a Panoptic Newtonian:
The Interstices of Heaven

Mount Laguna thrust up a cold spine from California's arid plains a short distance from famed Palomar. Amateur Astronomer, a community college science teacher, chattered his jaw to aching in an effort to generate body heat. The red light of the metal dome did little to warm him. Such is the lot of those who expose themselves to the mountain air for a peek into eternity. His tender fingertips sparked cold pain as he punched in the celestial coordinates. Tomorrow, Mr. A thought, I will bring gloves.

05347n2107.

Zeta Tauri.

Tien Kwan—Chinese: "The Gate of Heaven."

A shell star, simultaneously building and compressing layers of plasma in something akin to massive solar prominences. Some theoreticians felt that the star was going through a transformation, pupating from a merely large, mature star into a spectacular red super giant.

Mr. A stared intently, his whole attention on the beauty of the whirling nuclear furnace. A buzzing in his ears, the side effect of such intense concentration, pushed out the creaks and squawks of the steel shell encasing him. His shivering had stopped.

Fugue XXIX

"Oh, to see the eye of God."

Approximately 940 light years away, that same star (called Zeta Tauri by Amateur Astronomer) hurtled away from an insignificant speck (named Sol by nearby planetary inhabitants) at a speed of fifteen miles per second.

Not far from this slowly accreting star (un-named, incidentally, by its erstwhile orbiters) flew a craft, a large craft. A planet's population, their world since engulfed by the outer layers of the stellar giant, had been evacuated into this leviathan construct of metal and plastics. The planet's inhabitants had fled not only to escape the impending conflagration, but to pursue a pilgrimage, a religious pilgrimage—to find the Grand Deity. Selphenk was aboard that ship. He felt that God had abandoned them.

Selphenk worked in distribution. His job was to arrange mealtime for engineering. Every day he would calculate calories, enter data and prepare a mealtime production plan: times, drop off locations, portions, even the temperature of delivered foods as they sat waiting for a hungry mob of engineers to consume. It was boring work. Dull. Flat. He wished he could work with his friends Malph and Cophleeter—in engineering.

They met at mealtime, after Selphenk had finished his deliveries. Malph and Cophleeter welcomed the small talk—a break from number crunching and structural data formulas. Still, Selphenk would ask questions about their projects, always wanting to know more, though their social structure forbade transference once one was assigned his or her life's work. Dreaming was not forbidden.

They cut a diverse trio. Selphenk was small for his species, dark haired, with all three eyes a deep green, like the saltwater bodies of their old homeworld—consumed and evaporated now by the fires of their dying star. Malph was larger—significantly larger. In Selphenk's opinion

Malph should have been chosen for the guard: fair-skinned strapping chest; thick, muscular arms; long blond hair; two blue eyes and a pink central eye. One more genetic mis-step and Malph would have been an albino. Cophleeter could have been Selphenk's cousin, judging by her looks. Her long, raven hair, thin features and observant awareness lent a familial similarity to her friend. But her ice blue eyes, bright as young stars peeking out from a dusty nebula, set her apart from Selphenk. She was the smartest of the bunch—the best fit for engineering. The ship's thinking machine had made a correct decision when assigning her a post. She was always first to speak.

"Selphenk, you must quit moping."

"She's right," Malph interjected. "You'll never be happy if you keep on sighing and scuffing your feet along."

"Easy for you to say, you're in engineering. Did you ever think that the thinking machine made a mistake when it chose me to cater?"

"Selphie!" Cophleeter cut sharp. "You can't say such things. The thinking machine was assembled by the High Data Modulator, a position granted by God himself."

Selphenk lowered his head to the table, whispering: "But you can't tell me that the HDM is infallible. He's old, one of the oldest of our kind. Who knows what age has done to his mind. Besides, he's missing an eye. Maybe he missed something while keying in my number."

Malph seemed concerned. "That's borderline blasphemy, Selphie."

"It is blasphemy!" Cophleeter corrected.

"My faith has been destroyed," Selphenk pined. "I've felt down since we left planet. What has it been? Three, four hundred years now? It was such a lovely planet. Why did God have to let it be destroyed? I've gone down hill since. My parents' passing, the work assignment, everything that means anything to me has been taken or demeaned. What do I have to live for?"

"Don't even hint at such things, Selphenk. We are your friends—we will help you, help to restore your lost faith. In the meantime, have faith in us."

Amateur Astronomer drove home bleary-eyed. He was used to the exhaustion, however, and drove on like a robot—auto piloting curves and turns in half sleep. He had driven this route so many times, crawling up the mountain, out of the squalor below, to the telescope where he sat all night numb to the world, swimming among the stars. That was his real home, the interstices of heaven, churning with the galaxies, pulled in by black holes, dancing waltzes with the binary systems. Earth was no home. It was a prison. He longed for something better, beyond the mundane, the mortal—he sought God within the void.

The astro-theologian pulled into his cracked parking place, exited his rusty hatchback and entered his apartment, careful to avoid the crowd of gang-bangers at the corner of the building. His life didn't amount to much, but maybe it was worth keeping for a few more looks at the stars—so he steered clear of the crack hounds, the dealers, the discontent kids who had been spoon fed on video violence from infancy. No need to lose it all for an accidental shoulder bump or wrong look. Mr. A kept his eyes to the ground when in his own neighborhood.

The mail was sparse and depressing. Student loan payment overdue, phone service on the verge of being cut, alimony payment requirements raised and junk mail from the four corners of the globe. The newspaper didn't help much either. A newly-elected Republican governor: chances were high that community college education would take a hit. No doubt astronomy would be the first thing to go in the science wing. Nothing was sure. The signs were not good.

Maybe life wasn't worth keeping, Mr. A crawled through grave thoughts of the future, the present. He fell asleep on the couch, half covered under a midden mound of junk mail.

Malph and Cophleeter were good to their promise. It was slow work restoring their friend's faith, but they had made some progress in the first few time segments since their meal meeting. While in his presence they were always careful to notice, point out and accentuate the positive. Together they read the religious primers they had enjoyed while in childhood. Selphenk began again to find a sense of spirituality that had been absent—replaced by a cynical jadedness—for some time. It felt good to feel young again, fresh, open eyed, almost innocent, almost honest with himself and others. His depression was lifting.

They arranged to meet together for a meal.

Selphenk was on time, waiting as the food grew cold. Cophy and Malph were late, as was the whole engineering contingent. Selphie's annoyance shocked into panic, however, as a siren claxon erupted from the access tube leading to engineering. Within seconds firebots and safety-department workers in yellow radiation suits flooded into the tunnel, heading for engineering's central core.

The ruckus was incredible, worse than the rioting that broke out when the planetary evacuation was announced so long ago. Security police entered the dining area, pushing Selphie and the crowd of curious onlookers to the back of the hall as rescue workers brought forth stretchers strapped with the charred, broken remains of a small group of engineers. Malph was among them. Selphenk stood on tiptoe, looking over the security guards' shoulders to see Cophleeter, clothes singed, but relatively unharmed, bobbing up and down as she ran alongside Malph's stretcher. Worry stretched itself across her strained countenance. The group disappeared through a side door, heading for the ship's medical section. Selphie abandoned post to find his friends.

He jogged the whole distance to medical—a quarter of the colony ship's length away. The fear and anxiety coursing through him drove his body on, forbidding him to stop even long enough to start up a grav-platform and simply levitate across the gigantic inner cylinder of the ship. He was blind as he ran, not noticing the throngs of people, the vehicles, the pleasant artificial afternoon sunshine, not even the ludicrously huge windows on either horizon through which one might glimpse the passing stars. Everything was a blur, save for the occasional "Medical" sign and flashing directional arrow. Artificial darkness had fallen by the time he arrived there, a holographic star field in the middle of the moon-sized chamber mimicking the night sky of the homeworld. He would surely be punished for missing the administration of the evening meal. He didn't much care.

Fifty-seven stories up and through three hallways he found Cophleeter sitting in a chair outside Malph's room. She sat, exhausted, watching a news monitor mounted to the opposite wall.

"Cophy!" He stumbled, gasping for air. "Where's Malph?"

"Selphie, what have you done? You look terrible."

"I ran. Where's Malph?"

Cophleeter choked back her tears: "There was an accident. We were working on a new drive—something faster, incredibly fast, to get us to our destination, to God, more quickly. One of the fuel containers sprung a leak. Many engineers were burned by the flaming fuel. Malph tried to stop it up and..." She wept bitterly. "Selphie, Malph's gone."

Prickles washed over Selphenk's skin, his gut turned to rot. He stared blankly ahead, numb, all three eyes on the news monitor. Only after the initial roar dimmed from his ears did he come out of his haze and realize what was happening on screen.

The report bot recited its notes in a digitized monotone:

44-07:159
Rescue and security teams respond to emergency assistance calls from engineering.

44-07:170
Teams arrive, engineering reports leak contained, several casualties.

44-07:173
Victims medivaced, next of kin notified.

44-07:190
Rumors circulate of secret HDM directive regarding construction of a new space-folding engine. HDM office does not respond to inquiries.

44-07:220
Calls reach news monitoring central reporting that HDM support staff has not returned home from work, though release time had passed.

44-07:240
Rumors circulate of a coup attempt by HDM staff.

44-07:242
HDM staff issues statement to the press: "Members of the press and public, the office of the High Data Modulator greets you. Recently circulating rumors of a coup are unfounded. The staff surrounding his holiness, the HDM, have taken no actions to jeopardize his safety or health. To the contrary, the support staff is concerned now, more than ever, regarding the disposition and well being of his holiness, the HDM, as he assesses the seriousness of today's ostensive accident at our engineering facility. Thank you, our prayers are with you."

Fugue XXIX

44-07:243
A renegade news camera bot, some say in the employ of conservative extremists, breaks into HDM offices. We now go to video footage.

They watched the monitor, entranced. Whimpers and tears turned to gasps and shock: A long hall appeared before the camera bot. It flew past the marble walls, the statue niches and artificially sunlit alcoves, then turned sharp left to a set of heavy double doors. Unintelligible shouting could be heard behind the doors. The view turned, swept even more quickly down the hall, then out an open window. It blurred sidelong across a swatch of the colony ship sky, a quick panoramic view from near the center of the cylinder unfolding, then focused on a large set of dark tinted windows. One could easily recognize the back side of the hallway doors seen earlier in the sequence. The cam-bot's time display, lower right corner, read 44-07:243.

His Holiness, the High Data Modulator, stood in full purple-robed regalia, staring out the window directly at the camera bot. He smiled stupidly, like an imbecile that somehow made it past the euthanasia patrol, then his two remaining eyes twitched wildly beside his one empty socket. He dropped to his knees, laughing hysterically.

Behind him a group of sharp-suited onlookers shook their heads, seemingly at a loss regarding some grave problem.

Gil Shrenk Lipsis, HDM personal secretary, paced back and forth. "I warned him about the dangers—he would not listen."

"Warnings aside, the public will be outraged, and can you blame them?" a woman from an unseen corner of the room called out.

Solit Tenbron, Deputy of Public Relations, was next: "What can we do? We tell them the truth. Would God want anything less?"

Security Chief Tiling: "God doesn't have a potential riot on his hands. You remember what happened when we left the world. Sheer panic—thousands dead, a bloodied exodus, at best. At worst, the utter annihilation of our population. If word of the HDM's condition got out, the results would be catastrophic."

"The situation cannot go on like this," Lipsis said. "Sooner or later the public will find out. There is much we can do to distract attention from our problem."

"And what of the HDM?" the woman's voice again.

Lipsis was now standing beside the HDM, looking at the floor, unaware of the spying cam bot. He muttered something inaudible to His Holiness. The effect was immediate. The smile sloughed off his blessed face, a look of mixed fear and determination filling his eyes even as they emptied of jocularity. The HDM took three steps back, then ran full speed into and through the plate glass window. A siliconide aerosol sprayed out into the colony ship atmosphere, His Holiness's blood feathering out in white wisps from his shattered body as artificial gravity flung his lacerated frame to the ground some five hundred stories below. Lipsis looked down, enthralled by the tumbling body as it somersaulted to doom.

Selphenk and Cophleeter found themselves holding hands, palms sweating, as the vid clip ended.

Amateur Astronomer left for the mountains. He felt he needed a break from the city below, a ride through the rarefied air to clear the soul. First there was the 5 AM shootout across the street—the police fled, out-gunned—then a slashed tire before school started (it was finals day), then the news that his position would be cut to forty percent next fall. He drove to the observation dome, not on business, but on a pilgrimage, a search for meaning in a California that had none.

The cold seemed particularly numbing that night. Depression had deep-seated itself within his brain matrix, an emotional nadir shining darkly at the withered heart of his dying spirit-self. Physical discomforts seemed amplified as he struggled to prep the equipment for viewing. The night held little hope of soothing his agitated inner-being.

05347n2107: The Gate of Heaven.

And he felt nothing could be further from the truth.

Not even the stars could save his soul.

Cophleeter and Selphenk walked hand-in-hand to a nature park near medical. Their friendship, pushed over an emotional brink by Malph's sudden death, had churned over into something other. They were sad, oblivious to their surroundings, blind to the rainbow-hued rivers and falls, the shining chrome cloud bubbles, the blue luminescent animals that flitted from plant to plant like living message courier bots (only more graceful and tender); the couple noticed none of these things. All they saw were each other's eyes—the friendship, the mutual pain, sadness, consolation...and love.

Only the ship's warning siren pulled them from their romantic daydreaming. Others rushed too and fro seeking shelter or transport, mothers scooping up children in their arms, security police doing their best to maintain order before social entropy gained momentum into a downhill slide of looting and chaos. The two friend-lovers hid among a patch of tall plants, unsure of the cause for excitement and unwilling to be caught up in the commotion. They would take advantage of the situation to be alone—something not easy to do, given the cramped quarters of the ship.

The last whistles of law enforcement faded into the sub-inner surface levels of the ship, but a voice, a thousand voices unified, like an immense choir speaking in the same monotone, spoke out over every news monitor station within earshot. Cophy and Selphie jogged out of the abandoned park to hear the news bot's hollow voice echo out over the curves, streets and buildings of the upper levels.

45-29:243
Authorities warn all citizens to take cover in the lower levels in preparation for device ignition.

Cophy cupped her ear to hear, then: "No!"

At standard time 45-29:265 authorities will activate our new space-folding device. An HDM office directive states that the suicide of His Holiness proves that God is angry with our slow process to find and greet him. Thus the ship's new mechanism will be brought online in an effort to accelerate our search for God.

"No, Selphie, no. It hasn't been tested. How can we be sure it will work? Malph..."

Selphenk put a finger to her lips and smiled: "Faith...faith. I think I may have found it again. The bottom's dropped out, what have we got to lose now?"

"Each other."

And they held each other and smiled and wept.

Amateur Astronomer's eyes welled with wet. There was no justice in this world. Every interstice of reality seemed to dead-end as a money issue. His life, an inner voice told him, was not worth the carbon from which he was made. The heavens were a hell, an empty void of meaninglessness—just like his soul. Hopelessness, depression, engulfed him, wrapped him tight. Weary, he resigned himself to the final ride home. There would be no more. Nothing. The second hairpin down at 80 miles per hour would send him vaulting, flying like an angel, to embrace the rock bed below. The Big Sleep—where money did not matter.

He sighed and took his last look into the lens, the last view of true beauty before his plunge. But even this was fogged, smudged...or not.

Amateur Astronomer wiped the wet from his eyes. The glow inside his 'scope was just that; not a smudge, not moisture, not a product of depressed hallucination, but a real glow coming from within the scope, growing stronger. He checked the CCD camera to make sure everything was working as it should—it was; adjusted the focus—no difference; checked cabling—all OK. The light grew brighter, blinding, as it shot out of either end of the scope. He looked at the sky where yellow punched through the blue night, but the beams were so brilliant that he doubted his sanity. His head swirled. He hit the floor in a faint.

Sparkles of consciousness exploded in the darkness of their heads, awakening, resurrecting, as it were, their minds. Artificial dawn broke, the power flickers and burst waves of light from the space-folding device's ignition only quickly fading memories, images of another time, another space. Cophleeter and Selphenk woke in each others' arms, groggy, but with their erstwhile sense of loss disintegrating fast. They had survived the fold. But had they arrived at their destination, the place where God dwells?

Selphie was looking for something other than the static that sssshhh'd out from the news monitors. Cophy scanned the inner cylinder of the colony ship for signs of life. There were none. At least none of their kind. She stopped cold.

"Selphie, look up."

The panoptic gaze of God, glory in all its omniscience, shone down on them. An immense eye, larger than the ship's end windows, stared down over their world. They had, indeed, arrived.

Amateur Astronomer looked into the telescope, mouth agape. A tiny world, complete with cities, odd-angled mountains, clouds of animals flying through the little atmosphere, flitting from tree to tree. And just to the corner of his vision, where the imperfect lens magnified the scene below in a clear sliver of view, two creatures, bipedal, humanoid, stood embracing and staring up at him.

The suicide trip home vanished from his life's future history.

Money was unimportant now—and would never be a problem again.

The Night Factory

The guards at the stop-gate are too jittery from methamphetamines and cocaine. They bark directions in hummingbird gear, sweat cascading down their red faces, fingering their glossy submachine guns like psychotic killers looking for an excuse. You know they are. You are the inspector.

Up, out of the car and onto the vast desert courtyard they call a parking lot. Yours is the lone vehicle between the almost invisible concertina wire, the black-shrouded machine gun nests—a Kaba of death for each cardinal direction in this Mecca of arid nothingness. Above looms the warehouse, bare incandescent bulbs peppering the outside and above the beaming box immense twin smokestacks thrust into the cooling air impossibly high and jet black spewing darkness into the evening sky. Clouds flow from the shafts over the desert like a parachute of octopus ink, eclipsing the setting sun. This is the night factory. You check your indiglo watch and, as expected, your time zone turns dark on the planet face. You have a job to do.

The door squeaks of bending metal as the foreman—short of stature but mounted with muscle over muscle—leads you into the decontamination chamber where you don the requisite attire—black robes and a gas mask. You meet the support staff and exchange the usual pleasantries. One of the staff members was a schoolmate of yours. Her eyes are bloodshot and baggy, just as they were in graduate school. Aren't you glad you quit?

The chamber goes red and a sphincter-door rotates open. You enter the factory proper, fancying you are an Egyptian high priest entering a pharonic crypt. The ring of hammers sings a leitmotif of manual labor as you scratch check-off boxes with a thousand-dollar silver pen.

The workers are busy, arms flailing bone and flesh jackhammers, wielding their ball-peins with considerable alacrity. Workers busy. Check.

Beneath the blur of arms their withered gray bodies quake in rhythm with the hammer blows. They are incapable of hearing, though—eyes, mouths and ears are sewn shut with frayed brown twine. Safety equipment in use. Check.

The worker drones chip at a monolithic black crystal. Shards are gathered by leg-less dwarves who hand-walk the pieces down metal grill walkways toward a glowing red furnace. Here gigantic beings clad from head to toe in obsidian armor cast the calved crystals into the bellows-fed oven where fire pulverizes and melts the rocks into the stuff of night. Processing systems in operation. Check.

You smile, ready to leave early, when one of the chiselers takes flame, spontaneously combusting into a heap of smoldering ash at the base of the leviathan mineral. Transporters stop on their knuckles, looking at each other in bewilderment. The support staff looks down at their shoes, embarrassed by the faux pas.

There is no time to lose. You cast off the robe and tear the gas mask from your face. As you stoop down for the hammer your old classmate discerns your intent. She approaches with needle and twine and sets about saving the day. You pant through your nose as your lips are sutured, the heat of the furnace drying out your nostrils. The factory clanks and clunks fade and muffle into silence as your ears are pinned to your head. Your eyes are enveloped in blackness as the lids are sewn shut. You take your place at the cold obelisk—no one is above this kind of work—and feel the ringing sting of the hammer handle in your palms and wrist bones, the ache beneath the shoulder blades, the burning deltoids. You wonder, as you pound, how long it will take for them to find a replacement. You hope it takes a long, long time. There is work to be done here in the night factory and you have a job to do.

Bearing Seed

It is a spectacle.

A young man runs down the halls, near the lockers, beating his chest with his open palms. In each hand is a wooden block studded with dozens of shining nails. The blocks are strapped to his hands with wrestling tape. He winces in pain with each bloody thump of his breast, yet continues until he faints.

The counselor asks him "Why?"

"I am a member of a privileged elite. White, middle class, male. I am told that I must learn experience through suffering, lest I become ungrateful and weak."

The blocks are confiscated.

Next he is found running from classroom door to classroom door, kicking out the glass, then yelling obscenities at the teachers, the principal, the lunch lady, through a bullhorn.

The counselor asks him "Why?"

"I am an American teenager. Caught between my childishness and my blossoming sexuality. I am told I must rebel."

Fugue XXIX

The bullhorn is confiscated.

He hands out candy and snacks in the hallway during class, then throws great gobs of sweet foods and wads of money through classroom doors. A near-riot ensues at the school. News crews come to get footage of the chaos.

Again, the counselor asks him "Why?"

"I am a member of humanity, a brother to all who are of my species. I love, and must serve them all," he says, placing a pomegranate on the counselor's desk.

"Who told you this?" the counselor asks.

"No one. I gleaned this myself, through my own observations."

The counselor picks up the pomegranate, holding it in her palm, as if weighing the scales of justice.

"You are cured," the counselor says. "You may go."

"I understand," the young man says in a voice filled with conviction. He walks out, cured.

The counselor peels a bit of the pink skin from the pomegranate. She pinches the seeds between her forefinger and thumb, popping them, each one bursting like a tiny, watery heart.

The young man, while being interviewed by a news reporter, pulls a revolver from his coat and shoots himself in the head.

The Reverie Styx

Charon worked the winch, giving the diver enough slack in his air hose to comfortably descend the two hundred odd feet to the bed of the river. Malebolge, standing with cloven hooves planted on the deck of the boat, beat back the angry souls with whips that cracked like lightning, leaving flaming lacerations on their tortured hides. Others tugged and pulled at the wounded, beating them with flailing fists and feet until they, in turn, were flogged and bitten by more hordes of insensate wrath-driven dead. Amidst the chaos the demons cleared an opening through which the pressure-suit-clad figure dropped.

He slowly submerged into the almost impenetrable muck. Two high-intensity bullseye lanterns, one mounted to each side of his immense spherical helmet, cut through the sludge, the demonic fires penetrating the black into which neither mortal nor damned are permitted to peer.

The dismal ghosts did not regard him, did not notice as he reconnoitered, trident in hand. They merely sighed: "Tristi fummo ne l'aere dolce che dal sol s'allegra, portando dentro accidioso fummo: or ci attristian ne la belletta negra." Thick bubbles ascended unseen to the raging mob at the surface, spattering them with ooze, provoking them, feeding their violence.

Here all was gloominess. A lanky young man stared blankly down. His feet were only inches above bottom, but in his blindness he could not know—the river bed might as well have been a thousand leagues below. Near him a fat woman, black hair in a tangle around her face, slumped her shoulders and drooped her head, eyes closed as she gurgled the everlasting chant. Slightly above her and to her left a gray-haired wrinkled old man floated holding his withered legs up to his chest. His lips pressed against his knees as the words slipped from his mouth and percolated upward.

"I am a fisher of men," the diver thought as he approached the group. He pierced the gangly lad with his trident. "I have been given dominion over the fish of the sea." The youth thrashed about trying in vain to free himself from the barbs. The diver stuffed him inside a large canvas bag, then shoved the trident into the corpulent female, who opened her eyes in shock, too stunned to resist being put into the bag. "What man is there of you, whom if his son...ask a fish, will he give him a serpent?" He punctured the spine of the old man, who convulsed in a paroxysm of terror. "I am a fisher of men," he concluded as he rose to the surface of the Styx. His day's catch struggled in the bag.

High above the fifth circle of Hell and far from Virgil's forest a sparkling green bass boat floated on a Midwestern fishing hole. Three people were littered about the deck.

Zack's wrinkled father looked at his watch lethargically. The other two peered over the edge of the boat, waiting. "You told him thirty minutes, huh?" the codger asked Skinny Flat Top.

"Yup. His ten minutes of air should be up pretty soon. Still can't figure how some stupid fool who can't even read got so much money from his mama," Skinny Flat Top mused.

"Bitch," the old one hacked out a tuberculous cough before continuing. "I shoulda got that money in the first place, now we hafta go an' do this to poor old Zack. Not that I ever liked the little prick. Too mucha his mama's side in him."

"Shuttup, both of you," the tremendously overweight girl said, puffing her halter top out with the heaving effort it took her to talk. "Have some respect, boys. After all, I'm losin' Zack—my lovely boyfriend of two weeks." She smiled at Skinny Flat Top.

The old man joined the others, looking down into the murky water. "Should be any minute now. Let's see. A thirty-thousand dollar inheritance split three ways makes ten-thousand a piece. I think I'll pay off that trailer house and move."

"I'm gonna get me a pickup," said the bloated female.

Skinny Flat Top smiled wide. "I just want his scuba gear and the boat."

The pages of a Bible fluttered in the breeze as the old man reached for the book preparatory to a mockery of the last rites. They all laughed as an unnoticed black-flippered something floated up toward the surface near the back of the boat. A spear gun dangled from its wrist.

Loyal

Sunset rains in sheets on the glittering car tops like beetles rolling *Here* down the thoroughfare. Streetlight sentinels *I, we* vomit down upon the evening *Why am I* glowing asphalt. Sirens wail, *Where am I* engine roars as this vehicle rushes, *we* leaving others—SHOOOM! SHOOOM!—in our wake. *Here?* Radio voices cackle through static crackle "What's your 1020? Over." And the smell of alcohol swabs stings the nostrils *Mine? Ours?* Invigorating.

"Don't worry," the nurse told me, "you'll be just fine." I wasn't reassured.

"What's going to happen when we get to the hospital?" I asked, trying to sit up. The stretcher's restraining straps kept me from moving.

"Just lie still. We'll be taking you straight into the operating room. It'll be OK," she smiled professionally, as duty demanded.

I felt a sense of hope trickle into me, raising my spirits. I tried to hide the excitement in my voice. "Will we be separated?"

"The doctors will decide that," she feigned neutrality. I knew, though, that I one would soon be two and I was elated.

The blood-soaked bandage sandwiched in the connective tissue was evidence of Sam's attempt to separate us. My mind was a bit hazy after the attack, but I seemed to remember something about sitting down to dinner and Sam somehow grabbing a steak knife and jamming it into the bridge of flesh between our heads—I didn't know he had the strength or the coordination to accomplish such a feat.

I would not have been averse to any success that my brother may have had in his "surgery." I had dealt with this dolt for twenty-three long years now. I had ported his half-fetal, shriveled carcass with me since birth. No one should be expected to understand the psycho-emotional, let alone physical, burden of having him with me wherever I went, whatever I did. I steeled myself against the ridicule long ago, against the classmate jibes, the pitiful looks, the whispers around the corner. But against the loathing I felt for Sam there was no salve, no relief. I could not blame those that mocked me. Might I not treat one such as myself, such as Sam, as some type of circus sideshow freak had I been born twinless? Yes, Sam was clearly the source of my suffering, but not for long, I thought as the stretcher was wheeled through the gleaming hospital hallways. They had already begun administering the anesthetic before they wheeled me into the operating room and I...

Blue eyes *Bright* blue heads blue mouths blue gowns *It is so bright* bright white light and silver flashing slashing. *No, please!* Surgery suture scalpel slice. *Don't cut me asunder* flaying flesh and burning veins *we are brothers.* It hurts, it hurts it stings and aches and *bred from the same cell.* My brother sleeps on, oblivious.

"Suction."
"Suction!"
"OK, note how the parietal is fused. This will take a little muscle. I'll need the drill."
"Drill!"
"Drill."
"We'll start on the anterior, since that's easiest to get to."
"Suction!"

Buzzing fizzing bone smoky smell clouds the air. Hot blood cool air cold water flows over *I am not we* the bones. Blue robe pressing, *we are not me* pushing pressure on skull plates resisting. CRACK! *I am I* cracking echoing off the walls sets the body loose *I alone* lets it slide and slither away from the other, *I am me* the brother that was mine.

I am Sam

"Good morning," the attendant greeted me, setting breakfast on the tray. She pushed a button on my bed and I inclined, head throbbing more and more as it elevated. An emptiness, as if something was missing, told me that the operation had been successful.

"Thank you," I muttered, barely able to talk from fatigue. Time was a blur—I may have been sleeping for a nanosecond or for days. "How long have I been out?"

"The operation ended about six hours ago. Don't be surprised if you sleep a lot over the next few days. It will take some time for you to recover. You had best eat while you have strength. I'll get your dishes after you're done."

I tasted the soup—chicken—though definitely not homemade. I missed Mom's cooking, but it felt good to get something in my belly. Jell-O, Juice. No solids for now, I thought.

It was only when I finished that I noticed him in the bed across from mine. He looked pathetic. I could be handsome now without him as an ungainly protrusion from my skull. A simple hair graft and I could be dating, free from that misshapen bag of bones and flesh—that parasite. The possibilities danced before my minds eye: dating, driving, college...normalcy.

Sam would never be normal. Still I did not pity him, but disdained him. "Freak," I muttered as he began stirring under his sheets. I felt sleep coming on in waves...

    "'Hate you'?"

"Yessir, carved into the table, here."

"And you say the patient was found with the knife in his hand?"

"Yessir, it's still there. He's sleeping."

"Yes, I see. And his brother, Sam, I believe?"

"Apparently he slept through the whole thing, sir."

"Well, we will have to restrict the patient to spoons. Keep him on liquids for the time being. And, nurse? Please remove the knife."

No he wouldn't, he couldn't I say, but my body *Hate us together?* Stops the words I would give in my brother's defense. I want to help him, *hate you apart* to tell the nurse that he would never deface another's property, never show unkindness, *I hate you.* He is a loving person. Why do you think *know your thoughts, I do* he would do any harm? I will watch for the culprit *see them seethe them boil them too*—the criminal always returns to the scene of the crime.

"Good morning," I said. The nurse eyed me strangely. "Sorry I fell asleep before I had the chance to tell you I was done eating."

    She looked curious, like something I said did not sit right with her.

    "Someone will be up soon with a new tray and some food," she said coldly. "Be sure to take all of your pills."

    She left and I was alone with Sam again. Looking at him, I felt a twinge of pity. Maybe I had judged him too harshly. He didn't choose to be born the way he was. Perhaps it was Mom's fault? Poor mangled kid. He would never get to experience the things I would, would never date, never drive, never go to college. I was beginning to feel sorry for him. So harmless, so innocent.

The cafeteria worker brought up my tray. There were more pills than usual. I took them, then ate my meal, getting sleepier with each bite...

"Doctor! Good, you're here! I'm applying pressure to the wound, sir."

"Good. Let's get the IV hooked back up, we don't want the patient to dehydrate. Looks like we may have to dose him more regularly."

"Yessir, the bleeding has slowed. Should stop soon."

"He'll have to be fed and checked on more often, probably on the half hour. We can't have this sort of thing happening again. That's two bed tables he's ruined and this time he really hurt himself. What did he carve in it now?"

"'Use you Crazy', sir."

"Hmm. He's obviously destabilized. Post-surgical stress."

"How was the MRI, sir?"

"Fairly normal. Minor bleeding. Nothing that would drive someone to rip out his own IV to use as a carving tool. Does he have a history of mental health issues?"

"Nothing in his records, sir. There. I think we're ready to IV him again, sir."

"OK. Let's splint the arm as well so he doesn't bend the needle and infiltrate his vein. Oh, yes, and let's bump up the Stadol dose a couple CC's, OK? Thanks."

Perhaps there is something wrong with him, some kind of brain malfunction *Gotcha, gotcha!* He doesn't seem well. Maybe it was him *gonna getcha!* After all. For shame! It's almost unthinkable, *you are mine,* but it must be true. My brother—*I possess us* the guilty party. What would mother think?

My arm throbbed when I woke up. For some reason it was in a splint, immobilized. I had the hazy recollection of a dream, a nightmare, in which Sam clambered out of his bed muttering horrible things and hurting me while I lay helpless. A terrible dream—probably a side effect of the pills they had me taking.

As the fuzziness in my head cleared the door opened and my mother walked in. The doctor stood in the doorway and watched us for a long time. He took notes on a clipboard and whispered to an unseen companion in the hallway.

"Hi Mom," I said wearily.

"Hey honey. How are you feeling, morning glory?" she asked. Her voice belied great concern.

"Fine, just a little tired...and my arm aches," I yawned.

"You're sure you're all right?"

"Yeah, I'm OK...except for Sam..."

"What about Sam, honey?" she glanced across the room at little Sam, resting in his bed. He slept a lot, I was finding.

"I dunno, I just...just kind of feel bad for the way I've treated him. I mean, he can't help the way he is, but people loathe him because of his appearance." I felt my eyes water as I thought of how people would treat him without me there to serve as a buffer to the cruelty of society. I was, in some ways, a shield for him, a protector. Now, with the operation complete, Sam was stripped of his armor, left open to be a victim of man's cold-heartedness and fate's whimsy.

"Oh honey, Sam will be fine," Mom said in her reassuring manner. "Here comes your dinner. Take your pills, hon. Sam will be just fine."

I smiled at her after she fed me dinner, then lay my head down on the pillow. Mom looked sleepy too. She laid her head back and shut her eyes and...

"The patient is secure?"

"Yessir, he's in isolation now."

"Explain this to me one more time."

"Sir, the patient apparently attacked his mother with his own IV."

"How did he get it out? At least one of his arms was splinted."

"Looks like he used his free hand to rip off the splint and take out the IV. It must have caused some great pain, but who knows? In his state he may have been oblivious to it. Incredible how he must have fought off the narcotics—the brain is an amazing organ, even when it's not working correctly."

"How is his mother?"

"She's OK. A wound to the neck and a dose of Stadol. She's bandaged up and awake now, doing fine. Of course, we haven't told her yet that her son will be transferred to mental health for an indefinite period."

"I'll talk to her about it. How is Sam, her other son?"

"Sir, I didn't want to tell you this until we had more information..."

"Come on, Nurse, what's the problem?"

"...Sir, Sam can't be found. He's missing. Sam's mother and brother were taken out then one of the interns went to check on him and he was gone, sir. We have security looking for him right now."

"Probably looking for his brother. You know what they say about separating twins. Well, he couldn't have gotten far, he's almost immobile in that little body of his."

"Yessir. They will find him soon, I'm sure."

I am waiting, brother, *as am I,* though you can't see me, *nor me.* We are in agreement, *yes we are,* that you have done some very bad things *and deserve to be punished* for your actions. *We will exact* a heavy toll for what you have done *to our mother.* What? *You don't remember* doing anything untoward? *That's because it was us,* us. Yes, *us.* We, the judge *and we, the jury,* find you *guilty* of betrayal and *unfaithfulness, disloyalty.* You will be *punished, punished* harshly. Sometimes *life is not fair,* brother. Not fair *at all. The night nurse has left,* left us alone, and security *can't find us,* us. Here we come, *here, up in the air vent,* coming down. Let me, *me,* introduce *us,* us. I am Sam, *I am Sam,* we, *we* are SAM!

Precognitive Myopia

1. Klepto Willie's hand bleeding, glass embedded in the windowsill burns fire ants down to his cut up fingerbones. Tacks in his knees, involuntary arthroscopic rivets in punctured patellae prove someone, somehow knew he was coming. He disembeds the shards and spikes all slick with blood and thinks, think, think! How did they know? Who are they? Do they know I'm here now?

2. Phoebe Nesmith's mansion ripe for an estate sale, unguarded, hides wares and paintings and carpets under ghostly drop cloths, breeding canvas creatures throughout the house. A pilferer's playground, Klepto Willie opines as he cuts cloth to staunch his wounds. Gloves prevent fingerprints, but his blood is all over that side of the room. A challenge, to spoil the evidence against DNA revelations, confusing the genetic fingerprint. Willie is on task, but not stupid, so to the kitchen where he opens cupboards—the drop cloths aren't saturated yet, no trace of the stains on the pantry—but pots and pans don't help, not even Revere Ware. Above the stove, ah, there's the rub: flour and salt in abundance to dry up the mess. So he clambers up, missing the glow of the stovetop until his hands and knees cauterize in blue smoke. He hops to the sink, but the water is off—why would a dead woman need water? Willie whimpers then thinks of the cold porcelain toilet in the bathroom down the hall where he plunges his hands into the pot and ladles the liquid up to his knees. The smell of rubbing alcohol registers just as his spine freezes in pain, his cheeks numb

with the rush. He lays on his side and cries, a baby all over again.

3. Klepto Willie hobbles, but the task is done, blood all dry, mess B gone. The safe is behind a painting, just like in the movies. Willie smiles at Phoebe's portrait—she does not smile back. Metal instruments clop-clatter onto the floor and a tick-spin-tock-spin-tick later, open pops the safe. Inside bank notes and bond certificates, gold and an envelope stamped "CENTRAL INTELLIGENCE AGENCY."

4. Dear Ms. Nesmith,

Your request for "Project Runciter" documentation has been processed and filed. In accordance with the Freedom of Information Act, we release the following file. Sensitive information has been deleted in the interest of national and agency security.

Sincerely,

Jonathan A. Rolfs
Archival Department
Central Intelligence Agency

5. Central Intelligence Agency
"Project Runciter"

Agent: _____
Subject: Phoebe Camay Nesmith
SSN: ____-__-_____
DOB: __/__/__
Screener: _____

Test Battery: #4
Telep: 2 +/- 2%
Telek: 2 +/- 2%
Precog: 97 +/- 2%
Test Date: ___/___/___
Location: L49a
Signed: _____
1st Witness: _____
2nd Witness: _____

6. Dear William:

You have seen enough, now put the papers back. Take the bonds and gold, but leave me my dignity. Be a good boy.

Sincerely,

Phoebe Nesmith

7. Klepto Willie, addicted to stealing again, pockets the papers—can't help the taking. Up to the bedroom where the jewelry must be, thinking I'd better be quick, dawn is coming. Stairs crick-crack up the dark wood well and around the banister he thumps into the master bed, a canopy of gossamer over the sleeping plank all ghostly wavering. Now Willie, not stupid, is beginning to wonder, to ask is someone else watching? Not stupid, but cautious he turns on a flashlight to add to the moonlight bubbling in through the white-curtained windows. Was there movement or only the shimmer of silk under light? And why are the dressers all clear? Where are the jewelry boxes?

8.   To the closet he slithers, sliding open a door, then falls back all affright facing Phoebe's old dress, the one worn when she clawed out a young lady's eyes and was confined to an asylum. A trophy to dementia. The red-spattered hem sprawls Willie tumbling out backwards as a voice scratches out "Willie-Willie-Willie" and the flashlight is flung and spins round in the air, sending specters flying across all the walls and ceiling and dark wood floor. "Willie-Willie-Willie" and his hands itch with the burn, tiny glass scratching bone as he fumbles down stairs, broken neck and gurgling blood and the lungs stop at the bottom of the stairs, but the scratchy phonograph plays on in the closet, right where she put it before the time she knew she would die. "Willie-Willie-Willie-*SKRTCH*- I know you're here, Willie. Be a good boy-good boy-good boy."

9.   Sunlight filters into the stairwell, piercing Klepto Willie's buggy eyes, but they don't blink, just stare at the drop cloth-bred furniture beasties of Queen Phoebe's zoo, just as she knew they would. Sometimes you can see the future and, try as you might, still be unable to change it.

Hopeless: A Triptych

Emilie

Wee Emilie is wedged beneath the trailer house. Mommy's footsteps creak overhead, cutting through the muffled sound of daytime soaps blaring from the TV. It is stuffy and hot and she's peed herself and the sand grinds in her teeth. Her arms and face are covered with cobwebs and she thinks she feels spiders crawling in her hair. Tears and snot make the mess more messy, tangling her feelings up inside. Is she scared? Sad? Lonely? Uncomfortable?

That big black dog is barking, trying to get to her with those sharp teeth, but its head is too big to fit under the footings. Its yawping throws up dust that spews at her like canine dragon's breath—hot, smelly, dirty.

Something moves over her hand—red, with pincers and a stinger-tail. A scorpion. Poky legs scuttle across her arm then off to the ground where it turns, beady eyes fixed, pincers clacking and tail swinging like it's deciding where it wants to sting her.

She shivers, then stops locked still, unable to move as a new sound comes through the mucous-cobweb mess—a rattle and a hiss and wee Emilie sees stars in front of her eyes and she feels like she's floating and her tongue is numb and enveloping BLACKNESS...

The Headhunter

You sweat for two reasons. One, the undersized nylon suit is uncomfortable in the summer sun. Two, you are wracked with nervousness. You wish your head would stop aching, but the mere mental acknowledgement makes the pain all the worse.

A headhunter? You realize, as the air conditioned inside turns your sweat to stinking ice, that you don't even have a job from which you might be tempted, not a boss to threaten, not even a desk to clear. No one you know in this town has a job.

Headhunter. A pun, perhaps? A fanciful title? It says right there on the frosted glass "Edward Jean, Headhunter." Maybe the rumors are true... The faint odor of formaldehyde wafts in from under a door behind the secretary's desk. You are starting to realize the grisly truth.

Mister Jean opens the door and invites you in with a claw-like extended hand. He has not showered in days. Greasy wisps of black hair trail across his shining bald spot. You shake his hand, which buckles limp under your assertive grip.

"Have a seat," his voice scratches from too many cigarettes and insufficient sleep.

Only after you slide into the plush leather chair do you come to an awareness of the office.

"So, Mister _____. You are currently employed?"

"Yes," you lie, looking at the walls on which tattooed human skins are stretched over bamboo frames—a phantasmagoria of imagery: An elephant holding its tail with its trunk, a sleek black insectoid creature, a blue eyed faerie. A glass case behind Jean's desk holds the mummified remains of Siamese twins, joined at the abdomen. Shrunken heads hang from the ceiling by their hair or sit atop poles in the corners of the room.

The previously-faint odor of formaldehyde floods your burning nostrils. The air is cold and your suit is damp. Your stomach begins to ache.

"And what brought you here?" he rasps.

"I'm interested in...trophies." Liar.

"Hmm. How did you hear about us?"

"I have a friend in the industry." Bastard liar.

He smiles.

"And what experience do you have Mr. _____?"

"Well, it may not seem directly related, but I worked in a taxidermist shop for several years while I was in college." How can you live with yourself, damned liar?

Your stomach is upset, but you cannot pinpoint the cause. Perhaps your uncomfortable suit, or the mummified faces—once full of child-life—that leer at you, or your barefaced LYING.

Jean scratches notes on a yellow writing pad as you give your answers, prompting you with "Mmm" and "Ah." He squints his vulpine eyes in thought, then rises, extending that limp claw once again. His fingers, clammy and jaundiced from nicotine and formaldehyde, slide into your palm.

"Thank you for your time, Mr. _____. You answered all the questions correctly."

Hope rises.

"Your record is impressive."

You've got the job!

"Altogether too impressive, Mr. _____. Unfortunately we do not hire liars."

It is a long, hot walk home to your fat wife and young brat of a child. Plastic-windowed envelopes with bills waiting to be paid are piled on the dining room table, awaiting your return. There is a bar on the way home, or a bridge over churning water...

School in Nebraska

The pistol weighs heavy in my hand. My body shakes, slick palms against the plastic handle, chest numb, a slight tingle between the thighs. My fuzz-filled head wobbles with nerves akilter.

I look over each shoulder to check that the locker room is clear, then, in a moment of teenage bravado, spin the cylinder *ratararatara-ratarata*. .32 caliber bullets, rusted from age, whirligigging past the hammer, waiting for its fall. Waiting for the kill.

I saw what he had done to James. I knew something was up when my friend had walked up to the bus-stop. His parents missed the black and yellow jaw, a testament to the lack of attention in that home.

"What happened to you?"

"Ron got a hold of me—now he wants your ass in a basket."

I feigned sickness and walked home.

I lay in bed, trembling in the belly. The front door clicked behind Mom—I was out from under the covers before the car had started. I headed into my parent's bedroom, rummaging through the closet past old pornography and golf tees to a paper bag. The bag would have torn had I picked it up from the top, so I cradled the bottom with my palm, the weight of Grandpa's pistol and ammunition pressing against the flesh. I stared at the chrome instrument for a long time, nervousness slowly filtering out into a hint of power, like the tinge of gunpowder smoke on the air. I tried the bullets, 5 ball points smudged with rust at the seams, a shiny lead bead showing beneath the aged tips. Grandpa had bought this piece during the depression—almost fifty years previous. He had only used it once, to shoot a moose in the antlers, thus scaring it out from under the tree in which he had taken refuge from its charge. Grandpa would not approve. He would not understand. I shut the memories of Grandpa out of my mind. His spirit must not know.

A door opening startles me, the gun slipping back in the bag. It is Stephan—one person in this God-forsaken school I can trust a bit.

"What's up, man?"

"Ron wants to take me down."

"Yeah, I saw what he did to James. You better watch it."

"I've got a plan."

"Yeah?"

"I've got an old pistol. I'm going to buy some blanks and scare the hell out of Ron. I don't think he'll mess with me after that."

"Huh. I can get you some blanks."

"Really?" I am surprised, totally caught off guard.

"Yeah."

".32 caliber?"

"Sure."

"I'll pay you for them."

"No problem. Just tell me when you want them."

Stephan leaves me to my nervousness. The empty sounds of the locker room sound like prison cell echoes. The thought that had been lingering in the recesses of my mind surfaces: Jail time. Imprisonment in a cell, imprisonment in fear—what's the difference? If my cell mates knew I had shot someone, maybe they would leave me alone. Innocence strives for a voice, reminding me of those things that were good. My younger brother—looking up to me in every way, my girlfriend, the move to England, taking place only a month from now. Maybe there is another way. A coward's way, yes, but I had proven myself a coward already by successfully avoiding Ron for days now. The fear of the weapon takes over. The responsibility of death. The weight of murder. For a moment I think of turning the pistol on myself, joining Grandpa, getting out. Out.

Something—a hand, a spirit, an instinct—moves me to the trash can. I wrap the gun in the brown paper bag and shove it down in the garbage, ammunition and all.

Now, I am defenseless. I open the door to the scream of the last bell. Down the hallway, past the iron-gated side hall entranceways, through the glass doors, waits Ron. I can see him there, looking around for me, his back turned. Ron between me and the bus. So close to the bus. So close.

Waiting for Felicity

This time would be different. He refused to wait longer. Two hours he had stood, stiff in his tuxedo, anxious for the winsome Felicity Hammond to join him for their planned tour of The Bird Museum. The formal wear added to the already uncomfortable air, sodden and black as the sky beyond the charcoal towers and granite walls of the old Castle District. Statues held up the tottering spires and squat facades of buildings as far as the eye could see, a chiseled army of Atlases holding up the urban world. The stone was heavy with history, laden with numberless ancient stories of passing armies, threatening hordes, and the peaceful capitulation that allowed the city's century-old tradition of delicious decadence to persist. He shrank amidst the heritage, dwarfed by the enormity of the architecture, a lone expatriate waiting in the drizzle for his expatriate lover to appear and sweep the clouds away, gathering sunshine like some cosmic mass of light, a gravity of brightness.

Even the ticket she had given him, once bright red, now slobbered crimson dribble onto the cobblestones, a pool of blood-dye veining away to rivulets. It read, simply:

The Bird museum
Rare and exotic avians
Castle District

He blinked, blew the precipitation from the tip of his nose, then faced the door. An opaque window panel, bumpy, like crystalline spackling, prevented a view of the inside, but the black letters adorning the glass matched those on the ticket in word and font. This was the place, the time had arrived and fled, leaving him alone with pangs of impatience and doubt in his abdomen. He stared down at a puddle, hoping that the silver-grey ripples would calm to reveal his lover's reflection: boyish blonde hair over sky-blue eyes, short, slight and energetic, the rich smile that filled his chest with high emotion as she approached, with groaning emptiness whenever she departed. The mere memory of her image was not, alas, enough to sustain him. His soul was wan, sickly from her ill-timed absence.

A moment of lucidity shot the romantic from him. This was inane. He would enjoy himself, Felicity or not. He had stood in the rain like a street urchin long enough. Perhaps, he thought, he could unload the city's weight—and his sense of loneliness—within the museum. He turned the cold handle thrice, fingers slipping on the slick metal until he grasped so hard it hurt the palms. He entered resolute.

There was no doorman,
only a rusted metal trashcan overflowing with red tickets.
He threw his ticket on the top and watched as it fell to the floor in a
pink avalanche of paper.

Fluorescent lights throbbed above, though never quite in synch
with one another.
The walls were a sickly pale yellow, like a nicotine-stained
sepulcher.
Cigarette butts littered the floor.

The stench of ashtray brushed the musty air.
A dash of stale urine scent invaded his nostrils.

Fugue XXIX

Cold,
Wet,
Aching,
Tired,
Itchy.

The layout was simple: A long hallway, on either side glass cases mounted in the walls. Cobwebs softened the sharp metal frames that held in the case windows. A greasy film streaked the length of both glass walls. Muddy footprints dotted the center of the aisle.

Yellow Canary
*Serinus
flaviventris*

Almost androgynous. Your long lashes, thin nose and sharp chin barely nudge you into the feminine. What more could a man of *my* preferences ask...in a *woman*? You shimmering in a golden cape collar flapper, yellow feather headband and boa bobbing to a Charleston shimmy, the brightest star in the curling smoke of the speakeasy.

Bird of Paradise
Paradisaea apoda

Even the polished
brassy tones of the
band, however,
could not outshine
that smile. And
when I realized
you were smiling
at me, not past
me, the music
electrified me,
pulled me like a
4/4 time
marionette, spun
me to you. You
wrapped me in
your bright yellow
feather boa and
pulled me in.
Broadway was
never so brilliant
as that night,
never so beautiful.

A shattered wine
glass glistens here
on the floor.

Spoonbill
*Platalea
leucorodia*

To Greece, I
follow, New York
ice melting to
Aegean blue

Hoopoe
Upupa epops

water, Long
Island Iced Tea to
honeyed Pinot
Gris. You
dodged, evaded,
camouflaged
among the myriad
parasols and bath
houses, denying
our attraction.
But I am
persistent, I
pursued and won
on the beaches of
Crete, over the
minotaur's den,
beneath the
temple at
Knossos, the
goddess watching
over us in her
epiphany as the
Eternal Bee, as the
Fertility Bull.
There you
conquered me, a
goddess above,
introducing me to
the esoteric rites
of our passion.

Military Macaw
Ara militaris

Scarlet Ibis
Eudocimus ruber

A smoldering
smoke reeks
cannabis here
under a muddy
footprint.
Marakesh. Off
the ocean liner
and through the
famed market,
past hanging
r'bati carpets I
followed once
again, Arab
hawkers forcing
off their blue and
gold weaves, red
and cream florals,
as their half-blind
wives and
daughters stared
up into the blazing
sun, unaffected by
the glare, bathing
in the
resplendence of
Allah's
munificence.
Spices combined
with the burn of
hashish, my head
spinning as I
searched for your

red sun dress
among the veiled
faces. You stood,
your back to me,
past the white-
robed dervishes,
in a common sun-
baked brick
doorway. As I
weaved through
the entranced
dancers your face
came to view, that
smile, but now not
for me. He, HE
stood listening,
returning your
smile beneath his
waxed moustache,
ivory teeth shining
off olive flesh, a
smile of
familiarity, brown
eyes of lust and
anticipation
refracting your
blue—sea and
earth cojoined.
You entered arm-
in-arm and I
stumbled off
through the

wheeling
worshipers to
spend my weeks
in an opium den,
an anonymous
dullard connected
by the lips to a
brass pipe. I lost
myself in the
horror vaccui of
unemotive numb.

A half-used tube
of lipstick is here
smeared across
the crevasse
between wall and
floor.

Wandering
Albatross
Diomedea exulans

Mine again or
mere deception?
The leathern
masks, your
butterfly, my
scaramouche, hid
our true visages,
hid the tears, but
we knew. The
lamp posts and
hanging lanterns,

Long-tailed Duck
Clangula
hyemalis
(Vagrant south)

strung above the
courtyard dance
floor like a Milky
Way brought low,
made apparent the
truth. There was
no hiding in the
dimness of
starlight. Your
tired eyes belied
the facts: He had
used you, ejected
you to wander
again, migrating
northward to
Venice where you
sought solace in
anonymity, but
found none among
the gondolas,
above the stench
of decaying
waterways. My
desire was timely,
you told me from
beneath the wings,
coming to fruition
at the ball on the
eve of your
planned attempt. I
would not let the
canals have you.

My obsession
filled every
attention-craving
crevasse, healing
you, slowing your
flight from
yourself and
stalling your
plunge into
oblivion. We
climbed again the
jagged hills of
passion and joy, of
togetherness
among the maze
of wharfs and
bridges. Never
were we more
than an oar's
length apart.

Here the man
squatted to the
floor to pick up a
pair of elbow-
length black cloth:
Slender fingered
jet gloves, the
kind a woman
wears only with
pearls. He

pressed the silken
fabric to his
nostril and
inhaled, then
flung the
offending objects
from his wrenched
face, cursing the
yellowing air with
"The burn! The
burn!" as tears
coursed down
over his cravat
and cumberbund.

His blurred sight
lighted on the
glass case to his
right, at waist
level, except the
fire in his eyes
had pushed him to
his knees. There a
Black
Woodpecker
Dryocopus
martius
Tic-tocked its
beak against the
spider-cracked
glass, a broken
neck reward for

previous effort.
The head lolled
off to one side,
swinging back and
forth like a loose
pendulum. The
creature's legs
wobbled like a
drunken sailor's
scurvy-contorted
knocking knees,
all sense of kilter
gone awry, a
senseless avian
moron banging its
way to freedom,
to death. A sharp
crack to the glass
freed the shards to
flow down in a
glistening
avalanche,
severing the bird's
neck from its
wasted body.

The man squatted,
then knelt on the
floor, vomiting a
caustic bile to
match his burning
sinuses. His

Fugue XXIX

mouth's roof
sloughed acidic
down the back of
his throat,
watering eyes
staring down at
the bird's
decapitated body.
The last of his
strength shot
through his
quivering knees as
he brought
himself up from
the retch-laden
floor...

...to look up to
his left where the
convulsive death
throes of a
Common Raven,
Corvus corax, its
flesh infected with
a churning of
worms, mites
skittering across
feathers like trains
at a roundhouse—
confused, ever
turning to find

more reason to
scurry to find
more reason to
scurry to find...

His head reeled
and he thought, at
first, that the pale
yellow mist that
flowed down into
the glass cube
from some unseen
mechanism above
was a
hallucination
brought on by
dizziness. But
when the bird
bucked and its
eyes blistered, he
remembered that
stinging scent,
that burn, that
color of a mad
yellow miasma
billowing through
the air;
dichlorethyl
sulphide
infiltrating craters

Fugue XXIX

while machine
gun nests burst
starlight at him;
zeppelins
overhead and
bombs and friends
being shattered to
bits...

...like that glass case,
cascading body parts
to the sodden trench-
es beneath

and he groped in
that fetid stained
light of memory
for

the door handle:

Shivering,
Burning,
Crying,
Coughing,

He breeched forth newborn from the womb of The Bird Museum.
Sunlight flared off the wet flagstones of a vast courtyard.
All clouds dissipated as if blown away by the breath of the gods.
Bodies lay scattered across the plaza, some faintly trembling with the
mist of mustard gas rising vaporous from their mangled lips, others
completely lifeless, animation depleted.

Bodies of vagrants, mendicants,
the poor and the outcast, a continent of euthanasia.

The shadows rumbled, then burst forth in black and white, jolly, fat tuxedoed gentlemen emerging from beneath the dripping eaves into the sunlight, removing their gas masks with a hearty laugh as their wives and lovers cautiously stepped out behind them, unsure if the air was yet safe. Squads of black-robed, hooded boys rushed to the strewn corpses to heft the bone-bags on to stretchers, their young triceps flexing under the red swastikas emblazoned upon their funerary clothes. A polka flowed from a marching procession of musicians and the fat men and ladies danced as the next generation skittered off with the refuse of the last.

Pearls shone in the dazzle and the sound of popping champagne bottles reverberated off the colonnades as an immense cake, surmounted by the eagle of Germany, was rolled to the center of the courtyard by an entourage of bathing-suit clad young frauleins. An immense BOOM shattered above the music to surprised screams and laughter as the top of the cake opened to reveal Felicity, the most beautiful woman of the evening, clad in a tight black dress.

She descended the steps, then approached him, kissing him deeply, sharing the caustic sting in his mouth. Together again. This time would be different, he promised himself.

Over Alsace

Helmuth Bruderbund breathed fast and hard, wiping away the hot oil spattering up from the engine of his Fokker Albatross. The plane lurched beneath him, a bullet-ridden derelict, adrift on the ether, tugged down by gravity's tide. Flaming paper shreds and molten lead shards bounced off his flying goggles, coat and helmet as he disengaged and abandoned the doomed craft for free fall. The weight of the parachute pack spun him around backwards, forcing thoughts percolating through his head as he tumbled toward France below, consciousness fading.

She was beautiful, a blonde vision in blue dress. A glowing aura scintillated from her skin as light flooded the stage. Words slid forth from her platinum pure throat, her silver tongue, a sounding from that small misty tavern then echoing across all Alsace:

"Quelque chose de toi flotte dans l'air,
Qui me pénètre la mémoire."

A flash of stage light—no—the Sun, and the mist was gone. The Fokker vomited smoke beneath him as it headed for the fields below. France. Debussy's France. And Helmuth Bruderbund was about to become a prisoner of war, a shame to his country, to his compatriots at the War Academy.

"Shame!" His mother.

"But Mother, I love her."

"She is French!"

"I will marry her," defiant, like a good Prussian.

"I will not have you marry some French singing whore you picked up in a Gasthaus. Your father turns in his grave at the mere suggestion. Your inheritance is at stake, impudent young man..."

"Shame!" Cassandre.

"I have my family name to consider—a reputation."

"But I love you!"

"No, it must not be. I was foolish to think..."

"You are foolish! A curse on your noble family name."

Cassandre leaves. She will not return. Her voice haunts him, ever haunts him.

"Et mon âme, trahie er délaissée,
Est encor tout entière à toi."

The pull was sudden, painful. A jolt to the jaw and jerk to the arm and Helmuth knew the shoulder was dislocated. It burned in the back as the wind whipped his face cold, biting his skin. The sound of flapping silk reassured—the parachute had worked, he would live. A prisoner. But alive, at least. Or perhaps Cassandre lived in that village below or just down the road. Yes, she would forgive him, shelter him, harbor him from the enemy. All would be well.

"A curse..."

The sun glinted off a white-robed form in the clouds, a winged being, an angel—Cassandre, his love. No, another memory—Cassandre had committed suicide a week after her departure from Germany.

A blunderbuss shivered as Baelphoegele, the destroying angel—
Cassandre—
Shrack
Shrack
Shracked
the ramrod down the weapon's chrome throat. It tried in vain to
regurgitate
beryl,
onyx,
ruby,
gold:
The Grapeshot of Mammon;
then awaited the leveling of the weapon, the trigger pull, the shattering echo that heralds the final departure of its victim into the world of
the dead.

In the distance, propellers sliced into the world's skin, wings plowed
a field, flames consumed the earth-bound aircraft. Helmuth continued to fall.

Baelphoegele's—Cassandre's—smile disappeared behind a puff of
smoke as the thunderstick responded in discharge to celestial command, a crusader-king's ransom of flechette finding its mark on The
Fatherland's Iron Cross.

"*Gott**"

"*Ô bruit doux de la pluie*

Par terre et sur let toits!
Pour un cœur qui s' ennuie
Ô le bruit de la pluie!"

Return from Abaddon

Johnny Milkpodseed flung his progeny to the soil, sowing lacewing feathers far and afield, impregnating the barren black dirt with growth potential. His orchards were renowned for their spindly spires, tentacled branches writhing in the nether wind; slick bark oozing pestilence from cracked skin; shrunken human heads screaming pitiful, quiet, almost silent, as they hung shivering, a grisly fruit, from their bony branches. Now seeding time had come. Johnny, the greenest of thumbs, was introducing a new breed of pulsating sucker-mawed flower into the herbal mix—a soft-jawed cephaloflorapod meant to offset the knife-leafed concertina wire grass that surrounded his hundred thousand acres. His immense hooked nose bent before his gothic-archway spine. He looked down through red spectacles at the plot furrows. A withered Scaramouch of a gardener was he. "Excellent," he croaked to the empty air, drilling the last seed into the dirt with his cone-toed boot. "And now, water." He looked at his pocket watch and frowned.

The net was laid, barbs secured to the slime-covered hemp matrix—a web of hooks and stingers, of flaking rust and whale bone. "My, what a machine, a cloud of claws!" delighted Johnny, and secured a weather balloon to each corner with tow-head knots of human scalp. A helium shot and off with a "BANG!" the thorny snare ascended to the purple heavens above.

A cloud of white and scarlet—angels retreating from the War in Heaven. And their feathers molt, the wounded seep in a pinkening cloud of wings, robes and spears. The battle hard won, they long for the

Sabbath in which there is no weeping, no wailing, no gnashing of teeth, for war is hell and the guardians of Heaven have been far from their abode for an eon or more. From the brink of the bottomless pit they have crawled across the sky, a stain on the stars, smearing the spiral-armed galaxies in the background with their blood on the surface of night. Six wings each aflight and a head full of eyes and still they do not see the rising mess of net as it comes, as it rends their lacerated hides and folds them, a beaten platoon, to celestial muck, a churning flurry of gore on the dome of the world. They struggle using the weakening wisps of strength that remain, yet their struggle is vain and they fall, are fallen, are fallen.

Johnny Milkpodseed looked up at the void and smiled his crooked picket-fence grin. It began as a pink sprinkle, then rained down in crimson torrents, scarlet rivulets forming in the furrows carved by the fallen angels' wings. Spring had come and the nightshade farmer was glad for it. Already his flowers were chewing muck, consuming their way up through the moist soil, through the earth-fertilizing detritus. There would be a good harvest this cycle. Thank the heavens for rain. Thank the heavens for rain.

In the Place Where Suffering Was Not

The boys sat across from each other, legs crossed on reed mats, arms folded across their fat-laden abdomens, twin Buddhas, their almond eyes glowering darkly at one another, never blinking. Neither spoke, lest the encompassing drone of the eternal "OHM" that ran as a constant background noise be disturbed in "that place where suffering is not." Outside, rain dripped down through the palms, cascading down to the cherry trees and bamboo stands in glowing strands, like fireflies stretched from sky to mud. The pulsing drizzle pooled into phosphorescent faces that mewed disapproval in the indigo night, seven thousand tiny, watery voices, bubbling up gibberish, a doggerel of something resembling weeping, arising from their shining throats. Sooner or later in this timeless place, the boys knew, father would find out. He would hear the weeping souls and come to investigate. There would be trouble...and punishment.

"It is your fault," Sinistrum said silently, with his hands. A smooth, steady movement, like the Ganges' meandering in summertime. "You are clearly to blame."

"No. You started the contention," signed Dexter, his fingers and arms flailing like a wind-whipped Yangtze squall.

"It doesn't matter. It is dead."

"It is dead," replied Dexter, "therefore it does matter."

"Why?"

"It is father's creation."

Sinistrum nodded, knowing. "And we will be punished."

"Worms?" Dexter proposed.

"Worse!"

"What could be worse than being consigned to a worm's body for any number of lifetimes?" Dexter defended his stance.

Sinistrum dropped his eyes to the floor between them. Dexter's eyes soon followed.

Between them lay a small human figure, no more than a hand-height tall, legs akimbo, arms splayed, body bruised and scuffed. Something like a sperm, a sperm containing a fetus in its transparent head, hung from the little man's mouth: the psychoblast, that from which each soul is formed, that had been ejected from the homunculus' body at the time of its demise.

Dexter acquiesced. "You are right. There is worse. What are we to do?"

"Flee?" Sinistrum half asked, half ordered.

"No! Where to? This is the highest paradise, The Golden Realm. You know what lays beyond."

Sinistrum looked past his brother's head, his gaze racing through the open hut window, over the groaning faces, dodging the snowy-white moonlit cherry blossoms of the paradisiacal garden, then peeking through a tiny hole, no bigger than a gnat, that looked out beyond the jade walls that surrounded and protected their kingdom—their father's kingdom. On the other side, a perpetual motion of cruelty, decay, sterilization, and hatred. Every woman, every man unaware of aught but their own suffering. Ignorance colored their every move, and ignorance brought pain. They clawed over each other, groping with callused hands to be where the twins were, in the place where suffering was not. Through a hair-thick nest of thorns, naked they fought, scratching, biting, choking, bleeding, pulling to be the first to arrive at the jade walls where, upon touching the sacrosanct palace of eternities, their unclean flesh would slough from their bones and their bodies fizzle into vapor, only to be carried into the dark red clouds that churned overhead, mixing with the miasmic acids and venoms that roiled therein. There, after their souls had been infused with the most exquisite torments: soggy, itching, freezing, burning unrest, they would fall as glowing droplets to the ground to mix their miserable complaints with those of the seven thousand agonized voices. In time, they would seep through the grime, draining again to the bramble thickets outside where they would grow again to their proper size, regenerating into their former shape, only to be seized once more by the unquenchable desire to touch *those walls*.

The brothers looked at each other as a gong, brassy, yet soothingly pleasant, sounded at the far end of the long hut.

"What will we do?" Sinistrum's voice quavered. Fear widened his eyes.

"We will show that our purpose is one."

"Ah, that we are united." His eyes narrowed.

"And inseparable."

"Hence we could not have set father's experiment awry. Our fight was an event that could not have taken place. The results impossible."

"It is as you say, brother."

"Brother." The two smiled at each other.

HE entered, golden skin reflecting the glow of the outside rain, like an amber idol. A shining halo of tantric symbols, the sacred signs of power, hovered in the air above and behind HIS head, a floating crown of godhood. HE smiled the smile of ultimate detachment, the visage of the un-suffering casting warmth throughout the room.

HE waved his hand, gently, with circumspection.

"What has been done? What has become of my creation? Do not deceive me." The background "OHM" wavered, rising slightly in volume, drowning out the sound of the tortured rain's voices.

The boys waved their hands in unison, gesticulating a reply:

"Your creation should not concern you. It is susceptible to suffering, so must be cut off from this place."

"You understand, my sons, that you have brought upon yourselves punishment?"

"We understand," they said. Then, with their soft, plump, beautiful hands and fingers, they plucked out HIS eyes.

On the tops of the mountains, where the sounds of man do not reach, where corruption has little hold, if the wind blows right, you can hear the grunting aches and sharp, squeaking pleas for pity as they kick and trample his pronate body in that place where suffering is not...while the twin sons of Buddha await their eternal punishment.

The Universal Language of Silence

There exists a stark contrast between the stage and the back alleys behind a theater that only an actor can appreciate. The audience member moves from luxury car to reserved seat and back with little or no gray pavement between the plush red carpets. The performer, however, emerges from the musty clutter of the back stage onto a perfectly sterile dream world, a spotless fishbowl into which the audience peers, but cannot enter, dares not enter for fear of sullying the perfect illusion. Then, after the curtain falls and the dramatic energy has been siphoned and carried off into the night by the crowd, the spent actor or actress leaves the empty shell of character in the dressing room and walks through dark back alleys, past derelicts and stray animals, finally discharged from the stygian concrete chasms on to an arterial street, far from the dazzling lights of the theater's façade.

It is near these junctions of alleys and streets that the failed per-formers, the pseudo-actors, ply their métier in hopes of discovery by some famous agent, or at least in anticipation of a few glittering coins. Saxophone players scent the air with cool sadness, jugglers throw their wares to the sky and dance with gravity, beggars put on a show for pity-filled spectators. These miniature circuses line the avenues of the metropole, giving a sense of grim celebration throughout.

When I first passed the mime on my way home from a performance, I hardly noticed her presence. It was the next night, after the stage light blindness had left my tired eyes, that I caught a flutter of gray in the corner of my sight and stopped to watch the mute performer, ears ringing from the blast of music that nearly toppled me into the orchestra pit earlier that evening. Blurred gray settled into distinctive black and white, yin and yang torn from context, then quilted back together in the positive and negative striped shirt, the black hat, pants, suspenders and shoes of the modern-day harlequin. A single red rose blazed upon her left breast, shining from atop her heart, the only splash of color on her mono-chromatic form excepting her brown eyes and pink mouth. I was reminded of the old film in which a red balloon is carried through a black and white world, causing a ruckus among children wherever it travels.

No children were present at this mimetic performance—it occurred well after the sandman had dusted their little eyes. A few wandering couples, pairs of lovers out to enjoy cheap entertainment, were the only audience for the lone performer. She finished her melodramatic skit by bursting out of some invisible shrinking box, throwing her hands up in triumph, free of the unseen prison, to the applause of the nine or ten people who stood watching. The lovers proved their generosity to their partners by filling the mime's outstretched hat half to the brim with coin and currency. She smiled and signified surprise by splaying her fingers out near her widened eyes.

It was then that I recognized the face behind the white mask of makeup. With her shocked look a memory bubbled up in my brain, a happy scar carved into my subconscious. I allowed myself to be immersed in the romanticized past, if only for a moment.

Lorraine had the most contagious laughter I've known. She could optimize the most hardened pessimist, raise the depressed from the depths of near destruction—I should know, she single handedly pulled me from my darkest moments of self-annihilation, never missing a step through my emotional minefield.

Not only was Lori my best friend, she was the one who introduced me to acting. I, who had sent my tenth-grade English class into fits of laughter by misspeaking my lines, was a born actor, she told me, a natural. She saw the spark of the entertainer deep within me where I saw only shyness and easy embarrassment. Only after long coaxing and encouragement from her did I take a minor part in a drama club presentation at our high school.

My part, consisting of three or four lines of poetic drivel only tangentially related to the plot, proved a segue into the world of theater. I was intoxicated by the glare of the lights, entranced by the audience's subtle movements, only half seen in the darkness beyond the stage. Acting, I found, was a drug, an antidote to my self-perceived personal shortcomings. My body was not my own. It was a vessel, a conduit for the spirit of the playwright whose work I performed. It was proof to me of the old mystical paradox that one must lose oneself in order to find oneself.

The effects of my newfound avocation went beyond the curtain call, however. My peers grew to respect me, my teachers overlooked my policy breeches. In the course of two years I became an integral part of the popular crowd, standing alongside Lorraine as the cynosure of the school social scene.

We moved on to college together, my best friend and I, majoring, of course, in theater. Unfortunately our stay together was cut short. During our sophomore year Lori's mother became ill with cancer. My friend, my teacher, my coach, was crestfallen. She took leave from school and never returned.

Two years of intense study, followed by graduate training, afforded me less and less contact with Lori. I heard that her mother finally succumbed to the disease and that the devastated girl left our hometown to seek work elsewhere, though I never did learn her destination.

The look of shock resulting from my recognition of Lori must have mirrored the faux surprise on her chalky face. Her eyes narrowed into a squint, then opened soft again in recognition. Before I knew what had happened, her arms were wrapped around my neck, tears of happiness running white rivers down her cheek. As I embraced her a hundred questions raced through my mind, the most perplexing—*What cosmic providence has brought us together, two childhood friends found among a million strangers?*

I suggested she walk home with me where we could talk. My apartment was only a few graffiti-riddled blocks away. She did not speak, but, staying in character, shook her head, put the palms of her hands together and pressed the back of one hand to the opposite side of her face, imitating sleep. Fatigue showed under her eyes. I asked if I could meet her for lunch the following day. She nodded and, with her somatic gestures, suggested we meet at noon by a nearby hot dog stand. I agreed, thrilled by the prospect of reopening our friendship. My youthful hope that we might grow to be more than just friends was rekindled as I retired to bed. That night, Lori danced in my thoughts.

I was slightly embarrassed when I met her the following day. I had come in my street clothes, leaving my costume in the dressing room, but Lori was fully clad in her zebra suit, as I liked to call the mime's apparel. She curtsied then held up two fingers to the hot dog vendor. "Two? You want everything on those?" he asked. Lori rubbed her belly and licked her lips, nodding in agreement. He laughed and served up the hot dogs.

"Very good, Lori," I said. "I knew you were a good actress, but I never knew you could mime. I'm impressed. You've been doing this for how long?"

She held up five fingers of one hand and silently mouthed *five months*.

"You can talk out loud, Lori. In fact, I would prefer that. No need to

107

stay in character anymore," I said. I felt somewhere between humored, perplexed and annoyed by her refusal to speak. "It's been awhile since I've heard your melodic voice." I said smiling.

She shook her head *no*, waving a discouraging finger from side to side with a stern look behind her eyes.

My soft heart won. "OK, I'll play along for now, but it's been a long time. I was hoping we could talk, make up for lost time."

She rested her chin on her hands and batted black eyelashes at me. Her flirtatious smile drew me in like a siren's song, raising my hopes that perhaps a spark might still be kindled between us after our long absence from one another.

I spoke, she mimed and I learned a great deal about her life during my absence. I took the rest of the day off from rehearsing to listen to her wordless account. The interpretation was difficult at times. I wasn't sure why she couldn't just talk. But if it made her happy to speak without vocalizing I would do my best to accommodate her strange obsession for the time being.

After her mother's passing, Lori fled our small town and its stifling history of stagnation, finally settling here in the city where she could lose her sadness in the crowded streets, in the shade of tall glass buildings, anonymity providing a temporary salve to her pain. But being anonymous did not make her invisible. In time the city's predators found her, enticed and trapped her in a net of sociality and drugs, embedding their euphoric hooks in her depression, ripping her fragile psyche at their whim.

At her lowest point, when she felt the barbs might finally shred the thin veil of sanity which kept a total breakdown in abeyance, she happened on a mime team near the place where serendipity brought us back together. While others laughed at their antics, Lori wept for lost innocence, yearning to fill the void that had been cored out of her being, almost eviscerating her will to live.

One of the white-faced clowns noted her sadness and, with an empathetic frown and an outstretched hand, drew her back into the role of an actress, back to her first love, back to her Self. Among the silent she found her solace. They did not need to know of her anguish and didn't care about her past, so she hid her hurt behind the mask. Without attention to feed it, the pain simply withered and died in some quiet corner of her heart. She learned peace, calm, an ease of mind she had found nowhere else, where the outside world, even while looking in on her, could not intrude, where she could sequester herself, alone with silence.

I had never seen Lori so calm and content as she was with me that afternoon. She was always cheerful—before her mother became ill—but jumpy, non-committal, bouncing from search to search to search looking for some kind of inner satisfaction that always eluded her mercurial grasp. Now she was at ease, reverent, almost in the religious sense, like she had found something bigger than her self, something awesome, sublime. I wondered what could have touched her to change her so dramatically. It seemed that she had dropped all resentment and worry from her life and was finally at peace.

My musings were cut short as I noted the time. I excused myself—rehearsals for tomorrow night's show began early in the morning. I agreed to meet her at a local coffee shop the day after the show. I walked home oblivious to the smiles and pointed fingers directed at Lori and me. *Let them say what they will*, I thought.

Rehearsal was a debacle. I, as Cyrano, swung from a ballroom chandelier, rapier in hand, only to fracture my foot as I landed on the stage floor. The costume manager—the only person capable of removing the frilly folds and pinnochinose so that I could be examined—drove me to the emergency room as my understudy learned to leap—safely—from the light fixture. After an exam, x-ray and anesthetic the doctor put a screw in my foot and told me that I would not be taking such heroic roles in the future unless I wished the cane to become a permanent prop.

I returned to the theater and cleared my locker knowing that my acting career was in serious jeopardy. I was, in effect, a lame horse headed for the glue factory. Unemployment checks would come in for a few weeks, but after that I seemed condemned to work as a stagehand.

As I exited the alleyway, head and heart laden with angst over the future, something stumbled over my newly acquired cane, knocking me to one knee. Black and white moved beneath me as a mime hit the pavement with an "Ahhh!" and a bloody broken nose. At the sound of his voice, three compatriots, each a clone of the others, thrust an accusatory finger toward their downed comrade, faces aghast at the silence-breaking utterance. The crimson-chinned casualty held up a hand in self-defense, halting the others long enough for him to rise to his feet, turn heel, and flee from the group. They all ran in place, moving only a few inches with each step, in a ridiculous slow motion chase down the alley, the trio slowly gaining on the offender. Both alley and street were deserted in all directions, curiously clear of pedestrian and vehicle alike. I was sole witness to the farcical charade. The clowns' silent pursuit made me acutely aware of the noise of my own troubled breathing. Eventually the three pursuers caught up to their erstwhile companion, surrounding him, taunting him with wordless jest, then raining down blows and kicks near, but never touching, his head and torso. With their harmless assault they felled the outcast in the alley.

The scene troubled me deeply. While I was sure the victim was unhurt—no one ever really touched him—the trio of attackers started at my approach, running off and leaving the first lying among the alleyway trash, nose still bleeding a scarlet stream down his shirt. I approached with the intent of offering my hand to help him up but stopped short when I saw his condition. Lacerations and contusions peppered his face, wide cracks split across one cheek. Red froth bubbled from his unbreathing mouth, freshening the flow from his shattered nose. A rib poked through his shirt, white bone protruding from a black stripe.

My mind reeled as I replayed the scene again and again. No, I was absolutely sure that the attacking party never touched the man, yet his body lay limp at my feet as if slapped against a brick wall by the hand of God. Sirens broke the silence, echoing off the concrete as they approached from deep within the city. I fled in spite of the pain in my foot, not wanting to become entangled in a legal imbroglio from which I might not escape.

Sleep was fitful that night, the empty glare of the dead meeting my gaze just as sleep enveloped me. Morning broke as I lay in bed thinking back on the incident. *Why did the mimes attack their companion? Was it something to do with his accidental fall? Were they already pursuing him when he tripped over my cane—a gang of mimes chasing an interloper from their turf? Or was he one of them? How did he suffer such wounds—what was their source?* The answers proved enigmatic. I could not make sense of the scene. Perhaps Lori might have some answers.

She was easy to spot in a crowd. Her black hat shone like a dark beacon above a sea of blonde, brown and red hair. The sight of her painted face churned my emotions end over end—frustration and fear danced about my heart as if it were a maypole. A smiling tableful of giggling girls lowered their heads to share a secret, pointing at me as I took a seat opposite Lori. My discomfort grew, but I tried not to let my annoyance show. The last day and night had taken a toll on my patience, leaving me vulnerable to the little girls' immature jibes. I did my best to be strong—for Lori. Her lack of verbal response to my words didn't help.

"Good morning, Lori. How are you?"

She held two thumbs up and smiled.

"Things looking up? Wish I could say the same."

She thrust out her lower lip and rubbed her eyes with her fists, then peeked around the table and grabbed her ankle, feigning sympathetic pain.

I sighed, exasperated. "Lori, why won't you speak? More than anything I want to *talk* with you, to hear your voice."

Profound sadness showed in her brown eyes. She started as if to speak then stopped, shaking her head, and looked up at me as if daring me to challenge her silent determination.

I stood to leave, tired of the game. "Lori, I am truly sorry. I thought that we could renew our friendship—maybe even move on to something more. But I can't play these charades—I can't."

She stood, tears welling in her eyes. It hurt me to hurt her but the childishness had to end. I turned toward the door. A shiver crawled up the skin of my back as I heard her once-familiar voice for the first time since our school days—"No," she whispered, almost inaudibly. I stopped, then, gathering my stubbornness, walked out, looking back long enough to see Lori with her hand over her mouth like a preacher caught swearing from the pulpit on Easter morn, her face full of surprise—or was it fear? I walked on.

Days later I secured a part in a local community theater production. It was nothing stellar, but a role that would pay rent for the next few weeks and one that did not require foot-smashing acrobatics. The pall of dark emotion that had hung over me thinned and lifted—almost. Guilt pulled at my insides, condemning me for my treatment of Lori. I had been far too hasty and nasty to my old friend. How presumptuous of me to think we could reconnect without re-acclimatizing to one another. My selfishness had blurred my emotional vision, my egotism had left Lori truly mute—I did not know what she felt about her experiences, about her work, about us. She had done so much for me in the past. I owed her an apology and a chance to talk.

I took to the streets, questioning and looking, prodding street performers with promises and bribes in an effort to find my Lori. She was nowhere. The last anyone had seen her was the day I stormed out of the coffeehouse.

When I thought I had exhausted my search I met an old, silver-haired mime, a wise man among their ranks, I supposed. After watching his performance I queried him about where I might look for a lost mime.

"Have you called the police yet? Mimes are quiet and all look the same—easy victims in this city."

"No, I didn't want to bring the authorities into this until I was sure I can't find her."

"Her? Well, there is the mime school on 21st street. Have you been there?"

"No, I didn't know about it. Did you go to school there?"

"I went there for one day. Then they tried to get me to swear to secrecy, to swear to silence about the 'esoteric knowledge' they offered. They claimed that their techniques and style had been handed down from generation to generation in an unbroken chain for as far back as the first written record of clowns and even earlier—'from the days of Tubalcain, The First Entertainer,' I think they said. Of course it's all bunk—something about the 'eternal silence' and 'the sleeper who must never be awoken' and some other garbage. I kept myself out of all that hokey voodoo—they just wanted to look legitimate since they had no real credentials. They took themselves way too seriously, so I left when given the option to stay and be initiated or leave."

I thanked him for the information, excusing myself to continue my search.

21st street was more like a parking lot than a street. The asphalt and curbs disintegrated into rubble under my feet. Derelict cars and windowless vans spotted the pedestrian-free road, punctuating the long rows of generic brick warehouses with their rusting metal husks. The sky began to drizzle gray, muddying the notion of a distinct horizon, as I entered the decaying building under the ancient wooden sign that read "Mime School."

I had brought a picture of Lori in my wallet. Anyone seeing it would recognize her even now—age had treated her with forgiveness, saving its wrath and wrinkles for me. A few men in full mimely regalia sat on the stairs inside the main entrance. I showed them Lori's photograph and asked where I would find her. They looked up at me with stern disapproval, holding their index fingers to their mouths. They did not speak, but I imagined them thinking *you fool, be silent!* They handed the picture back and pointed up the steep stairway.

I ascended the stairs, unsure of what it was that I looked for. As I looked up vertigo overtook me and it was only by gripping the handrail that I prevented myself from vaulting backward into space. Every few steps sat a mime. The steepness of the steps gave an impression of painted porcelain figurines stacked one atop another, unsmiling, unemotive, staring down at their own feet or their neighbor's silk hat—it was impossible to tell. I wove my way through the mass, occasionally stopping to show Lori's portrait. The viewer unerringly gave the same reaction, vacantly pointing upstairs, always upstairs, without a word. I wasn't sure whether I was being led to Lori or simply being passed up an ever-more-cynical bureaucratic ladder—an exercise in Kafkaesque futility. After climbing the dim lit stairway until my thighs burned I finally arrived at the top—there was an end after all. A thick oaken door twice my height, twin masks of tragedy and comedy carved into the brass handles, loomed before me.

I turned the cold handles and walked through, shocked to find myself in pitch darkness as the door closed behind me of its own volition. I stood in a sensory vacuum—a place devoid of sight and sound. The room didn't even have a distinctive smell. It was simply there—or not there, I was unsure which. I had walked into the void.

Had I been led to the wrong place? The generic men on the steps seemed sure that she was here in the room at the top of the stairs. I remained motionless, the swooshing of blood in my temples and the rasp of my breath the only sounds to desecrate this sanctuary of silence.

Just as I was becoming used to the sensory deprivation, dazzling light spilled into the room from some unidentifiable source, shocking my eyes with visual stimuli. Bare white walls spotted with blacked-out windows surrounded a jet black stool upon which Lori sat. Her face looked strangely stiff, eyes unblinking, lips unmoving. It was only after stepping closer that the head-numbing truth was revealed. It was not Lori's face that stared wide-eyed from her head, but a faux face painted in black and white over the featureless blank where one would expect eyes, nose, a mouth. The skin above her chin palpitated like a goldfish in open air, gasping for breath, soundlessly screaming, mocked by the caricature of a smile painted where once was an orifice. False eyes showed a slight bulge where something organic rolled underneath a thick layer of tissue. A dent fluxed in and out where her nose should have been, desperately struggling for air.

My lungs burned from screaming, but my vocal chords emitted no noise in that place where sound was forbidden, where air did not carry one's terrified cries. I ran to the doorway and threw open the doors, splitting asunder the words that had appeared in red letters on the gargantuan black door—"Behold the punishment of one who dared oath silence, then broke the sacred promise with her whispers." I stumbled down the open stairs—hardly noticing that they had been abandoned by the army of mimes—screams exiting my throat only as I burst out of the building. But my throat was so raw, my tongue so dry from exposure to the dessicating air, that barely a sound came out of my gaping mouth, not a thunderous shout, but only...a whisper.

Kaleidoscopes of Africa

"It has always been the fate of new inventions to have their origin referred to some remote period; and those who labour to enlarge the boundaries of science, or to multiply the means of improvement, are destined to learn, at a very early period of their career, that the desire of doing justice to the living is a much less powerful principal than that of being generous to the dead."

Sir David Brewster
Credited with inventing the first kaleidoscope in 1816

Object 1:   A fossilized giraffe femur, 18" long, 2" in diameter, discovered by Belgian archaeologist Jurgin Joachim, 22 August, 1898, on the west shore of Lake Nyasa, in what was then Nyasaland. The outer surface of the bone looks to have been hewn with an adze or other chopping instrument. Microscopic analysis shows miniscule flecks of obsidian, invisible to the human eye, embedded in hatched grooves cut lengthwise along the bone's shaft. The interior of the bone appears to have been core-drilled, again with obsidian, making the bone into an entirely hollow tube. When discovered, the inside of the fossilized bone tube held several hundred brightly-colored pebbles, diamonds, and bits of shell, each approximately .5 mm across. None of the pebbles come from the area, nor are the shells from indigenous species. The nearest habitat of the relevant shellfish species is Antarctica. The pebbles are likely from the Indian subcontinent, the diamonds from Angola.

Exhibit 1:   A diorama, recreating a scene witnessed by German anthropologist Heinrich Horstmann in the rainforest of eastern Belgian Congo, 1904. A group of Bemba elders sits in a semi-circle at the mouth of a deep cave, all staring at an arrangement of highly-polished iron shards, the fragments set in such a way that they reflect multiple images of one another. Immediately outside the cave a young man stokes a small fire beneath a *Tabernanthe Iboga* shrub, the smoke causing a cloud of thousands of gold-banded forester butterflies (*Euphaedea Neophron Neophron*) to take flight over the polished iron pieces. A half-empty basket of psychoactive roots containing Ibogain alkaloid sits next to the elders.

Object 2:   Brass kaleidoscope, 8" long by 1" in diameter, belonging to the late British explorer, Doctor James Widdekind. The object chamber of this instrument is filled with tiny dried arctic flower blossoms suspended in whale oil. This kaleidoscope was discovered on the body of Dr. Widdekind, who had been overwhelmed, while traveling through German Togoland, stung to death and subsequently consumed by a massive tide of fire ants, as evinced by the entirely flesh-less skeleton of the late doctor and by the presence of several dead fire ants—still well preserved—in the view piece of the instrument.

Object 3:   Wooden Kaleidoscope, 6" long by 2" in diameter. This instrument, constructed of maple, bears a carved inscription, in Arabic, of these lines from a traditional West African poem:

As the sun by day, so the moon by night

Breaks forth and gleams, lets our herds go to pasture.
Where once it was cold, the chill's now departed.
See—is there aught as bright as the moon?
Gentle one gliding aloft in the heavens.
Not hard to describe—like a flufflet of cotton.
Break from the clouds, set thyself in the sky
'Twas Allah appointed thy journey, thy grazing.
All the world knows it's the truth I am telling.
Gentle one gliding along on the breeze, in all the wide world none
with thee
Can compare.

This kaleidoscope belonged to Ali Mamadu N'diaye, a Tukolor corporal of the *Tirailleurs Sénégalais* who received it as a gift from his commanding officer, Lieutenant Lamine Chardigne, only days before N'diaye was killed, along with all but thirty members of his company, during a German night-time assault on Dixmude, Belgium, in 1914.

Object 4:   Platinum kaleidoscope, commissioned by Debeers LV, belonging to central African Dictator John Mungwane. Chips of ruby, emerald, opal, sapphire and diamond provide the object chamber elements for this piece. An etching around the eyepiece reads "Best regards, J.F. Kennedy." It is suspected that Mungwane's assassination in June, 1971, was carried out by a CIA operative under orders from American President Richard Nixon.

Exhibit 2:   An excerpt from an account given to the UN war crimes tribunal, 1998:

"...we ran into the village church, hopeful that our neighbors might

take pity on us in God's sanctuary. I had to step over several bodies to make it through the chapel's doors. I crouched near the altar, praying for deliverance, as was everyone who was crammed into that little building. We could hear the machine guns outside, but were relieved to hear them stop, until something came crashing through the stained glass window, showering me with glass. Someone in the middle of the crowd screamed "Grenade!" and an explosion threw me to the ground. Bodies flew over me and blood spotted up onto the broken stained glass window, staining Mary, Queen of Africa's dress. The sun shone through that window, spraying colors over everything—the candlesticks, the altar, the bodies, the blood…"

Frenzy

I stand outside the mushroom cloud, shards of sandglass raining down on my back and shoulders. The crowd roars, T.V. monitor heads at full volume, fists raised, clenching sponsor's beer bottles. True. Hordes of people show on their screens, gatherings of yet more monitor-headed mutants on theirs, ad infinitum. They had come for flash and blood, spoon-fed violence at a photon-fast refresh rate.

We had given them vengeance shootings—execution style; children caught in cross fires; talk shows ending in splintered chairs and a flurry of security guard fists. We crucified The President, buried congress in a suffocating deluge of money-market fact sheets and stock exchange ticker tape. Still the people (Jone's and Nielsen's) scratched and screamed for more, insatiable. We plastered the country with strip malls, put smokes in their children's mouths, "A credit card for every wallet." But on they wailed: "Feed us, feed, feed..."

Finally, when there was nothing left to give, we gave them us, sacrificed in a nuclear conflagration for their viewing pleasure. Only I remained, the button pusher.

Now they are coming for me, their T.V. monitor heads registering only static, snow. Satellites fall like rain from the sky. I await my fate as they turn on each other, on themselves, switching dials, clicking remotes, looking in vain for their satisfaction. But they only find static. Hungry, ever hungry.

Matriarch

There sits the Matriarch, naked, piloting the zeppelin. An anachronistic blob, a Willendorf Venus save for the sniper rifle [Mauser 7mm] in one hand, a plate of Twinkies [Flour, Sugar, FD&C Yellow, etc] in the other. Smoke chokes the behemothic hag, particulate remains of the krupp-gunned city below. Her two cronies, LeBlanc and LeFevre, push bodies over the sides of the cabin.

Twenty carcasses dangle from ropes. From a distance the dirigible is a Portuguese Man-of-War, tentacles thrust into the blackened urban jungle. Most of the corpses are uniformed, all hail from the city in ruins. The mayor, his cabinet and a dozen war heroes twist and bump, medals and ribbons and golden keys-to-the-city snagging on the wreckage of the metropolis.

LeFevre is caught off-guard when the tugging begins and goes vaulting over the edge into the crowds of famished children waiting beneath. LeBlanc watches as his comrade disappears beneath the mass then resurfaces a clean skeleton moments later. Blood covers the children's lips as they pass the bones hand-over-hand to a hill of gleaming fossils. LeFevre's remains become a part of the mound, as do the hanging heroes and cabinet—stripped to the bone by the starving youth.

Engines strain, fizzle, pop and the zeppelin sags toward the city's blasted spires in a shower of sparks, a cloud of hazy diesel. A slow rumbling sun setting among brick towers. The fireball fades to soot and LeBlanc looks down blister-burned at the approaching arterial streets. A surge in the crowd and atop the wave crest a tall, gaunt figure in gray, medallioned and decorated through a hundred wars—the militia general, the last adult leader of the cannibal child-army, leads his crawling troops toward the dilapidated craft.

The Matriarch stands and waddles to the side overlooking the mob, cradling her rifle like a baby, the Twinkies are all gone. She flips up the man-sight, adjusts for distance and brings the gun to her shoulder. CRACK! and the smell of gunpowder stings LeBlanc's nostrils as the general falls stiff back into the churning mass. A bustle and a shiver and his bones are body-surfed onto the fossil pile.

LeBlanc rises from his crisped hands and knees.

"You have dispatched the enemy, my queen, but your defeat is sure. A pyrrhic victory, after the mob throws you to the bone hill."

She turns, the leviathan turns and, tossing the gun to the city, caresses LeBlanc's face and hair. A thick-lipped smile creases her face as her minion tastes electric fear on the roof of his mouth. Sweat courses down over her fat folds.

"My wayward child—you forgot—I am the Matriarch."

And she consumes his head.

The children shout: "HUZZAH!" as she steps down from the dirigible's wreckage. Mommy's home. Victory is achieved.

The Butterfly Artist

Now, 200 years after The Crash, the world began to cobble itself back together. Man had taken to the air a second time (or third if those eons old parchments of Atlantis and Mu can be verified as authentic) but the crystalline sphere surrounding the planet, protecting its surface from the poison ether of space, was closed to penetration and exploration. Connections, however, had been made and the words inter- and multi-national were again entering common parlance, as the words nuclear conflagration, genetic warfare and imperial capitalism had immediately following the apocalypse known as The Crash. And, as has been typical of this world's history—for time has proven the cyclical nature of human endeavor and failure—the Dark Continent lagged far behind the other lands across the seas. Only the cities of Jannsburg, Kampala, Cairo and Ngome housed any appreciable technology, and most of it, as one must suppose from the battle-scarring of that immense continent's central and western regions, was military technology left over from countless campaigns and battles, thrusts and counter-thrusts, a blood-bath of diluvian scale. Culture—in the Northern Countries' sense—was also lacking, except in these sprawling metropoli. Proximity to key trade routes had, through geographical fiat, destined growth and the accretion of civilization in these areas once again, though in its rudest permutations, as it had been time and time again.

The sun set over Ngome.

Clouds, still laden with the toxins of the last wars, billowed across the sky from the southern sea.

The Ballroom

The girl in the smooth leather butterfly mask was his perfect counter-point: Long red curls to his straight, shoulder-length black locks; confident, upright spine to his sagging shoulders; bright, full smile to his thin, unemotive mouth. Beneath the sparkling wings he could make out her finely-chiseled features, no doubt an inheritance from Roman invaders generations ago.

A sullied half-skull mask shortened his long face, hid his high cheekbones, darkened his green eyes to her blue. In all respects they appeared a morphologically suitable couple: The butterfly and the skull; fire and ice; she, he; life, death.

A dance together, introduced by the man's friend, Neville Whitaker, confirmed his suspicions. She danced like the monsoon—winsome, but with authority. And like the tropical storms that brushed the coast that night, there was a hint in the atmosphere of a far off whirlwind whipping the sea into a froth, electricity in the air, though only a gentle rain fell on the mansion's rooftop. He felt that she led the dance, though his thin-fingered hands pressed against her firm ribcage, against her warm palm.

It was she who spoke first over the awkward, mistake-infested strings of the quartet. Good musicians, good artists of any trade, were difficult to procure in these parts, so far from the cooler, more affluent and educated north countries. Her voice seemed to smooth the squawks and rakes of decidedly amateur bow to string.

"And so, my Saint Vitus, might I ask what breeze brought you to Ngome? I gather you are a traveler. At least in my twenty-two years I have not known of your presence—and I know all the whites of Ngome by association or reputation, masked or unmasked." Her words, taken from the context of her inflections, implied aristocratic aloofness, but her voice belied honesty, forthrightness. He felt that the naked chandelier might betray any attempt to hedge or embellish, so he spoke openly.

"I am indeed a traveler. I recently returned from across the river with Doctor George Chelsea."

"Chelsea," it was a statement, not a question—a statement tinted with animosity. "Chelsea. And how might you have served an old, fat entomologist in the jungle?"

"Doctor Chelsea hired me on to draw and paint illustrations of his specimens in their natural habitat before collecting them for his display boards."

"How noble of him," she stated flatly, "to show his appreciation for beauty before administering death. He is a true colonial: 'tame the beautiful savage, kill him if you can, then build your empire on his bones.'"

She shook her head from a daze, her voice again inflecting but betraying a certain lingering animosity. It seemed to the man that she felt great disdain for the noted doctor. "Most artists are driven away from this land because of the climate. It seems that dandies and mosquitoes don't mingle. You may well be the first to venture past the Yamazi River without crawling back shaking with ague and angst. Perhaps. Or not."

He was unsure whether to feel flattered or insulted. Her words fenced with his fluttering emotions. Guarded now, hopeful then, parry, feint, riposte. She spoke of the nobility of the artist while castigating the stupidity of starving for art's sake; spoke in elated tones about the beauty of another's dress then slipped in thinly-veiled attacks on the unsuitability of such fabric for the tropical clime. She seemed a velvety sea urchin, a diamond among spiny shards of glass—still the man in the leering death mask listened to her more intensely as the night and their conversation wore on.

Emile Beckwith—the voluntary revelation of her name went contrary to all decorum at such anonymous events as this masquerade—was born in Ngome, the only child of Charles Beckwith, ambassador to the local "Big Men," as the tribal chiefs were known. She had been enmeshed in the local color, accompanying her father on his diplomatic forays into the country around the fortress, playing with the blacks' children as often as they would permit, sometimes drawing down the ire of village elders who deemed such interactions inappropriate. "The strength of a culture," she surmised "may be shown by the hedges it plants around its taboos. Though a culture with too many taboos must, of course, be stifled, blind to the beauty of change."

The music ended for the evening (mercifully, the young man thought to himself) and, as tradition dictated, all present teasingly revealed their faces. Surprised gasps and giggles erupted through the candlelit ballroom before the hostess announced the end of festivities and wished her guests good night. The skull wearer, enamored of the complex Miss Beckwith, presented his card: Chadwick Giles—illustrationist and artist. She placed the card to her lips, smelling the scented cardstock: Cinnamon and rose, the East and the North come south.

"My thanks, Mister Giles. Are you staying here in Ngome?"

"For a time, yes. I am to help Doctor Chelsea catalog his newly-acquired specimens. I suppose it shall take some weeks before the work is complete."

"Excellent. Then may I be so bold as to invite you horseback riding? This Thursday, perhaps?"

"But, Miss Beckwith, your father."

"Mister Giles, my mother is a widow. You need not seek my father's permission. Thursday?"

"Thursday, though it has been some time since I have held a crop."

"Thursday," she smiled. "Our farm is located two miles west of the river, north of the road leading to Anjema."

"Toward Anjema. I look forward to the excursion, Miss Beckwith."

Neville Whitaker woke to find his roommate up before dawn, staring through the mosquito netting that protected their room from trypanosome-infected bugs.

"Chad. What are you doing up? There's a good hour of sleep left in the night."

"I cannot sleep, Nev, and it's your fault," Giles responded without blinking. He stared off at the bare moon, lost in thought. A deep involuntary sigh gave him reprieve long enough for him to turn to his friend. "Neville, I must thank you."

"Do it after dawn," Whitaker muffled from his pillow.

"Stop joking, Nev. I'm serious. That girl you introduced me to last night..."

"hnnn?"

"Emile Beckwith. Intriguing."

Neville flipped over. "I'll say. She's a strange one."

"She's beautiful."

"Oh, touché. She is that. Only she has weird ideas."

"Such as?"

"The notion that your squatters ought to be allowed to sleep in your living room, for instance. Or her insistence on the free nature of men—all men. It just goes against all notion of proper order. As if we don't need stable hierarchy for civilization to succeed. She's a strange one, all right. Intriguing, as you say."

"I gave her my card."

"You're bold, Giles, I'll give you that. Did she throw it back in your face? She tends to do that to the local boys."

"No. She accepted. We are to go horseback riding anon."

"Anon when, Sir Lancelot?"

Chadwick smiled and threw a pillow at Neville. "Anon tomorrow, foul jester!"

"You see, Chad, that's what I mean. Tomorrow! It's just not done that way. Where's the false coyness, the mechanically fluttering eyelids, the nuance, the wait. I mean—not even a word to her father, I suppose."

"Her father is deceased."

"Technically speaking, yes," Whitaker smiled. "No, really, she's not normal."

"I know."

"And neither are you, obviously. How did you ever survive childhood in Kinderzeit? Things being so strict there."

"That I don't know."

"And you won't know unless you do your commissioned paintings," Neville stretched his back and arms. "You do have to pay for a ship back, eventually."

"Eventually," Giles slapped his palms to his knees. "Yes, you're right. Time to concentrate on the day's work."

"Chad?"

"Yes, Nev."

"That girl is nothing but trouble."

"We shall see."

Papilio Odius

"Papilio Odius, my boy—the gold of this expedition," Doctor George Chelsea squinted through the magnifying glass, careful not to mar the white skull marking on the black butterfly's back as he pierced it through with a specimen pin. "You have no idea how much the metropolitan museums will pay to display this little creature."

"No sir," Giles replied.

"Well," he adjusted the pin a bit, "with your share you will have paid for this trip three times over. It's amazing what exotic items fetch on the northern markets." He turned his balding head toward Giles. "That is, if you illustrate the things properly."

"I had best get to work, then, sir."

His hand shook. The lip of the ink jar tinkled with the tip of his quivering quill.

"Chadwick!" The voice of Master Kerrick, his art instructor, echoed in the adolescent section of his brain.

"What is this refuse? Can you not draw what is real? You are far too imaginative to ever be a proper artist."

He dipped the quill and poised it dripping over the parchment. Black ink splotches bled red to blood.

"Life. Life, young sir Giles," Doctor Siltree, family friend, artist, veterinary surgeon, held a straight razor over a bleeding sheep cadaver. "This is what is missing from your art, my boy. If only you could, you would, capture life! Then you will achieve the recognition you so crave."

The surgeon lowered the instrument, deftly lacerating tendon from bone with quick swipes of the blade.

"But how? I've taken all the classes, I've learned from the best teachers, I've..."

Siltree held his hand up to Giles' mouth, almost magically causing the words to freeze at his lips.

"Simply live, young Chadwick. Live."

The ink spread through the paper's capillaries. He thought it formed a skull in the negative, a black bone box grinning lip-less as if charred in some conflagration, mocking his inability to coax realism from the borderland between the medium and material of ink and paper.

To live—this is why he took Chelsea's offer and left his homeland. To live.

The ball dance mask joined the other skull, staring at him in mockery from it's hook-home on the wall.

The butterfly girl filled his vision.

"Thursday...west of the river...leading to Anjema."

"To Anjema."

Beckwith Road

"Is it safe?" He brought the white horse alongside her grey-spotted mare. The tropical sun reflected off his steed, causing him to squint from bright-blindness.

"Perfectly," she smiled.

"But I have heard that there are wandering bands of miscreants out here, beyond the government's reach. Ka-something."

"Kabilari."

"Yes, Kabilari. Shouldn't we take precautions?"

"Precautions? Perhaps I mistook you for an adventurer. Or are you just another trembling pansy intellectual, bold from the armchair, but fearful to leave your ivory tower?" She teased him, winking.

"Ms. Beckwith, I am concerned for your safety."

"I will be fine, Mister Giles. This is my home, remember. If anyone should fear the unknown, it should be you. Besides, there are no Kabilari operating in this area. They are all to our west, well in the interior. They rarely come into these hills and then only to raid for food."

Giles had read as much from the literature provided him on his long flight to Ngome by airship:

Official Government Publication
3417X9I22

A

TREATISE

ON THE

QUESTION

OF

THE KABILARI

....

Distributed by The Ngome Department of Public Affairs

....

Introduction

While every effort has been made to provide **Ngome**'s visiting travelers and tourists with a pleasant experience during their stay in our fair country, some may share concerns regarding rumors they have heard regarding the infamous **Kabilari**. Most of these rumors are unfounded, the fanciful imaginings of pseudo-historians whose ignorance of the subject serves to harm the reputation of the Ngome Ruling Body and rob our out-of-country visitors of the chance to enjoy the pristine beaches, rolling wooded hills, fine food and cheery native servants of our home. This pamphlet is a humble attempt to dispel such rumors. Armed with the knowledge provided herein, the traveler might safely and confidently enjoy his or her stay in and about our wonderful city.

A. Misconceptions

1. Kabilars are four-armed mutant mountain gorillas.
2. Kabilari are carefully organized, politically motivated groups of

natives seeking freedom from white colonial rule.

3. Kabilars prefer human meat to practically every other type of food.
4. Some Kabilari possess weapons of high technology such as lasers, energy grenades, etc.
5. Kabilari operatives live among the inhabitants of Ngome, mingling in their midst.
6. The government of Ngome wishes to hide the truth regarding the Kabilari.

B. The Truth

The Kabilari are the degenerated descendents of a tribe, known as the Boula, that once held dominance over the whole of the interior through a network of raiding and slaving. The Kabilari's fierceness as warriors cannot be disputed, though the internecine bickering between various Kabilar factions has prevented the bandits from uniting their efforts and organizing an effective fighting force.

The reason for their infrequent raids on police posts bordering the rain forest regions can be summed up in one word: Jealousy. More than anything, members of the Kabilari wish to live as whites. Even their primitive brains can comprehend the luxury and comfort that our larger brains have afforded us—the things that hint of delicious decadence. One must admit that we might sometimes take these accoutrements of culture for granted, leaving the lazy native with some sense of entitlement to the fruits of our labors.

Electric lamps, running water, fine clothing, automobiles, shining jewelry—these are the things the savage craves. When an unprepared traveler falls victim to one Kabilar, arguments over the victim's finery are sure to erupt both within the group itself and with nearby Kabilari. In essence, the Kabilari are thugs.

C. What to do if One Encounters a Kabilar

1. Do not panic. All blacks can smell fear. Kabilari have a certain acumen in applying this sense.
2. Give trinkets. Beads, shoelaces, shiny objects—all these items can be used to appease and pass a Kabilar. The surrender of these goods might save your life!
3. Do not engage in political discussion. The natives lack of logic might lead to confusion and entrapment.
4. Do not believe a member of a Kabilar. They are not to be trusted.
5. After you have successfully passed a Kabilar by proffering them your goods, notify the nearest government office immediately. Be careful to note the time and place of the encounter and be prepared to answer a battery of questions regarding the Kabilar's demeanor, appearance, behavior and direction of travel.

TOGETHER WE CAN STOP THE KABILARI SCOURGE!

Ngome Department of Public Affairs

"That must have been a long flight, indeed, to give you enough time to be brainwashed by such drivel," Beckwith said, staring off into the wall of leaves that rose and fell along the hills of the bridle path.

"You doubt the veracity of the government report?" Giles asked, incredulous at her impetuosity.

"Don't believe everything you read, my new arrival. Ngome is known to obfuscate what some term 'real.'" She paused, listening to the quaking leaves bustling in the sunshine. "Enough. Tell me, what was your métier before Chelsea hired you?"

Giles looked skyward with a pained expression. "I studied art, as you might guess. My family did not have the means to send me to school, so I worked as I studied."

"And your work was?"

Giles shifted uncomfortably in his saddle. "I was an assistant keeper at our local zoo."

"Zoo?" her face flooded with puzzlement.

"Please don't think it odd. It is an honorable enough profession, and I only did it to make tuition. Besides, it gave me the opportunity to study animal shapes, shades and anatomy in depth..."

"Zoo? What is this zoo?"

"The one in my home town of Kinderzeit."

"The what? What is this zoo you are talking about?"

"Zoo?" Giles stifled a laugh, not wanting to embarrass her. "A zoo—a place where wild animals are kept for scientists to study and for the public to view and enjoy, a place to preserve endangered species—this is a zoo."

"Is it like a jungle, then?"

"No, it is like a city for animals of all kinds. They are, of course, kept behind cages lest their natural instincts depopulate the specimen collection or the zoo's visitors suffer injury."

"Collection? Then the animals are dead, preserved, like Chelsea does with his butterflies. This zoo is some kind of sepulcher-city for wildlife?"

"No, the animals are very much alive. I know, I had to clean up after them."

"Alive in cages? That's savagery!"

"But the cages are there to protect them from each other and to protect visitors."

"Protect? Animals are supposed to attack and defend, to eat or be eaten, it's the inexorable law of fang and claw. To keep them caged—this must rob them of their souls. Freedom. Animals, like humans, need freedom. It is the nature of the world."

The smile faded from Giles's face. "But freedom must be dictated by someone. Why not the most intelligent species?"

Beckwith turned her horse around. "But it should be done with compassion, as with my mare. I let her roam free, feed where she wills, groom her. She, in turn, allows me to ride when I need her."

"I see no difference between your relationship with your horse and mine with the zoo animals."

"Cages?" And she shot off back toward her homestead, galloping away from Anjema.

The sun was dropping from its zenith when Giles caught up with her. She sat on her still horse in a shaded defile to one side of the dirt path. Something immense lay in the border between the road and the thick forest, a humungous black shape, as large as two horses, half in, half out of the floral wall. Flies clouded the air over the mass while maggots writhed yellow across the creature's fur, causing a shimmering effect over the area. A rotting stench steamed upward, filling the road with a wavering miasma that intensified the atmospheric scintillation.

Giles pulled up alongside Ms. Beckwith, stopping short of the death-zone. Putrefied air wafted up to him—the smell of his overheated horse doing nothing to help matters. He felt bile lurch into his throat, burning the esophagus with searing acidity. The other rider did not flinch.

"What is it?" Giles asked, hoarse from his burning spetum. The blood-matted fur of the carrion bristled slightly in the breeze as a thin layer of dust encrusted its gore. The creature's impossibly huge limbs were entwined in morbid self-embrace. The morass of rigor mortis caused Giles to count again and a third time—three, four, five and six limbs. Four tree-trunk arms and two piston legs, robbed of animation by the gaping bullet holes sprayed across the beast's immense chest. A face, simian, almost human, stared unseeing into a void as black as its rubbery skin.

"Oh! An ape! Four arms. Shouldn't we report this to the constabulary?"

Her voice wavered, eyes watering: "Someone already has. Don't you see the wounds? Five bullet holes and there, burn marks from electroshock rifles. Government troops did this to her."

Giles started to ask a question, then fell silent. He prodded his mount on at a trot just as a fly stung the young man in the nape of the neck.

Emile Beckwith sat in the saddle watching flies infest the mutant corpse for a long, long time.

Bloodmilk

"Giles, I like the preliminary work you're doing on the Papilio Odius specimen—though it is in the wrong color."

Chad did not want to upset Chelsea's pleasant mood, so did not reveal the "preliminary" to be a blob, a splotch, a cosmic mistake. He "hmm"-ed uncomfortably, hoping that the conversation would turn.

"I would like to give you the opportunity to come out to the hills with me tomorrow. We are collecting a number of specimens—though none so valuable as our little skull-emblazoned friend. I feel it might help you to see more of the insects in the wild."

The illustrator rubbed the back of his neck where the fly had stung him the day before. The bump had swollen and burned itching whenever he touched it. The physical discomfort matched that within his mind. Was Chelsea implying that his work was not good enough? Had he recognized Giles' mistake as such and dropped a hint that he knew so? Giles decided to take Chelsea at his word, though doubt raced through his mind and his face flushed red with fear that he might well lose his employment.

"Yes, Mister Chelsea, that would be fine."

"Good, then meet me tomorrow after tea on the road directly south of Beckwith mansion."

Relief flooded through Giles' head, though the bump still ached. "The road to Anjema?"

"The road to Anjema," Chelsea smiled a greasy, thin-lipped smile, looking like some humanoid toad. "I see you are getting to know these streets, Giles. Good. Ngome has a way of enveloping visitors. I'm glad you are finding your way. I'll expect you tomorrow at noon."

"Tomorrow at noon." Giles scratched the back of his neck and exited the office.

The bold red stripes of the Bloodmilk Café were an obvious anomaly, even in the cosmopolitan montage of Ngome's market square. They provided the only architectural splash of color in an otherwise bone-white courtyard. The sparkling square seemed to focus and magnify the heat of the lime-washed heart of the city. As Giles left the pulsating crimson of the Bloodmilk after a fattening lunch, he slowed his pace to absorb the images and smells of the marketplace. Myriad black faces peered out from brightly-dyed kaleidoscope cloth, a smiling calico menagerie of robes and shawls infiltrated by the odors of peanut and palm oil and heady spices from across the eastern ocean. A few, dressed as Giles in the dark suits of the northern literati, seemed sullen and aloof, keeping distance from their chromatic peers as if the commoner's colorfulness belied leprosy or some other virological contagion.

Giles had been warned that disease might be a concern here. The water was filthy and the close compaction of so many sweaty bodies into a great carnal agglomerate lent itself to the spread of illness. Even in his native temperate clime the convergence of so many disease vectors would be cause for concern, so much more so, then, here in the tropics. The flurry of hand shakes, hugs and kisses exchanged between members of both genders created a veritable germ mill. But the friendliness itself—utterly alien to his cultured bias toward formality—was contagious. Giles saw more smiles under the market stall canopies that day than he had in all his childhood in gray, rainy Kinderzeit. The stalls were akimbo, on the brink of slumping over, but the joy in the air buoyed the sagging overhangs as if it shouted "Keep up! Be of good cheer! You are among friends!"

Song broke out in the far corner of the square, away from the Bloodmilk. Skirts swirled in a sparkling whirlwind to the plunking and thumping of instruments new and strange to the foreigner's ears. Customers left the unfortunate peddler's stalls with cries of "Nzi! Nzi!" while women's voices ululated past him like streams of hiccupping locomotive whistles. He turned to watch the glistening bodies flow past, then looked to the café for a reaction. Moustached whites peered out from behind news gazettes with pursed lips, disapproving and annoyed that their political contemplations should be disturbed by such a trivial matter as a song. A cool breeze spilled over the roofs of the square and on to Giles as he turned his head back towards the stall-keepers, one of whom smiled and shrugged his shoulders as if to say, "These things happen. What can be done? You might as well enjoy yourself!" then left the stall for the moil.

Giles stood, transfixed by the spectacle, ignoring his nagging conscience, which told him there were preparations to make for the next day's expedition. He slowly walked closer to the gyrating crowd, noting a small group clad in white robes that seemed to form the hub of the human wheel, then penetrated the fleshy circle, weaving between dancing, sweating bodies to get a better look.

Halfway to the group in white, Giles felt the air whip around him in a frenzy. One of the robed figures held up a small bundle of cotton cloth, eliciting an outburst from the entire crowd, who shouted in unison: "Nzi Mkubwa! The Great Fly!" Then, as if blown away by the breath of God, the crowd scattered, ebony tendrils penetrating the streets in a flood of excitement.

The white-robed sub group ran out of the courtyard at full speed. Giles followed their wind-snapped cowls, wondering how a bunch of cloth could elicit such a strong spontaneous response from a common market crowd. The white robes passed through alleys, up, then down stairs, under the pedestrian bridges that arched over the corners of buildings, then around the ledges of dwelling-place roofs where hookah-smoking elders and laundry women mulled about. As the day wore on the buildings grew higher until, at last, when the walls and minarets of the pumice-like city threatened to push upward beyond vision, the group stopped in the middle of an empty alley. Giles was thoroughly lost. Giles did not care. He peeked around a corner to watch.

His attention was focused on the bundle that the six men—for he could now see their black skin shining under the robes—placed on the snow-white cobblestones between them. The only distraction to his peeping was the intense pain that seemed to radiate from his neck, where he had been bitten days before. A large bump had formed there, causing him to loosen his cravat to avoid the burning that now erupted from his nape. The pain increased to a point where he thought he might faint, but he held on to his concentration as the scene unfolded before him.

The men clapped their hands and stamped their feet in unison on the shadow-cooled stones. All chanted that strange phrase that Giles had earlier heard: "Nzi Mkubwa, Nzi Mkubwa," never taking their eyes off the cloth bundle that rustled in their midst.

No breeze moved the fine cotton—no outside agency was responsible for the movement of that cloth. The chanters' intensity and volume grew in response to the increased liveliness of the cloth until, finally, two immense black globes, the size of lawn bowling balls and surmounted by antennae, poked out from the baby blankets. Beneath the fly head was the smooth body of a human infant. The newborn struggled to get up on hands and knees, then rolled into a sitting position, shedding the cloth and revealing the rest of the underdeveloped white body, digits just separated from one another and umbilical cord freshly fallen. His—for it was a he—clear wings glistened and dried in the cool shade, the protective fluid invisibly evaporating from their crackling surfaces.

Wings buzzed with effort as the fly-headed fetal body strained against gravity and levitated into the air before the smiling eyes of the men. The multi-faceted eyes espied a perforation in the city skyline. He rose through the opening and faced west, toward the interior.

flee, Flee, FLEE! Engulfed Chadwick Giles—a blur through the streets and spires of Ngome. No matter where, you must simply GO! The word exploded in his brain, sending prickles down his spine to numb the acid boil protruding from his neck. His vision streaked, shallow breaths rapid-firing as sweat spattered from his body at full sprint, always looking up and over his shoulder for the mutant Insect Sapien that he knew was hovering somewhere, a black speck lost in the sun's glare, perhaps, or concealed within a cloud or behind a tower or within a circling flock of carrion-birds, all of them looking for a pile of filth and decay in which to thrust their beaks, their probosci.

Fugue XXIX

The fly-baby's minions must be scattered throughout Ngome, Giles thought. The city itself seemed to breathe conspiracy from its impure white walls. Behind the bright facades an unnatural breed had somehow conceived and birthed an abomination, a twisted, mutated, hideous offspring that patrolled the skies above the gleaming coastal gem. Though the hovels and hallways, the staircases and casements might provide shelter from the eyes above, that same urban structure provided obfuscating walls, dark shadows, and odd-angled corners behind and within which the agents of the fly-thing might hide. The sun was setting in accelerated motion—soon the conspirators would be free to wander the night streets in the open, performing whatever hideous acts they wished under the lamp of the moon.

A turn, a bump, a scream and fruit rolling over the cobblestones. A shout, a shaking fist, turn down an alleyway and across the now-deserted market square as night falls and finally, Giles' room and collapse. Fainting sparkles and black out escape!

Beckwith Revisited

The salty smell of sweat warmed Giles' nostrils. He woke groggy, unsure of where he was. His skull mask looked down at him with empty sockets, the angle of the sun through the window alerting him that it was near noon. He quickly changed into his khaki traveling boots and pith helmet for the expedition then threw his artist supplies into a carrying case and headed for Chelsea's suite at a run.

A note pinned to the door notified him that he was late and that their caravan would wait on the northwest outskirts in anticipation of his arrival. He followed the crude map scribbled on the note and ran to the rendezvous—the bridle path immediately adjacent to Beckwith Mansion. As he approached his attention was pulled away from the waiting group and toward the estate. With each step he continued to scan the grazing fields, the stables, servant quarters (empty of squatters) and the immense plantation-style house that sprawled westward, up and over a smooth-mowed hill. A flash of curtain revealed a shock of red hair—Emile Beckwith watching the loitering porters, soldiers and Chelsea. Her face appeared intent, serious, determined, analyzing the small crowd. She let drop the curtain before Giles could catch her attention with a hand wave.

"You are late, Giles!" Chelsea yelled, red-faced from effort.

Giles jerked his head toward the sound and ran faster.

"We shall be out past dark now. Here," the plump professor shoved a hard cracker into Giles' sweaty palm. "I presume you have not eaten breakfast. This will suffice." Giles choked down the dry biscuit without the benefit of water.

The hike did nothing to slake his thirst. Giles wondered how the over-weight Chelsea could forge ahead of him at such a brisk pace and how the soldiers and porters behind could keep apace. Most of the day was spent walking over dusty ground—far beyond the place where he and Ms. Beckwith had turned back, far beyond the now-vanished ape corpse, all six limbs no doubt swallowed up by the jungle or its inhabitants. West they plodded through rivulets of sweat, closer and closer to the interior.

Late afternoon turned the sky raw yellow when Chelsea raised his hand to halt the parade at the crest of a flat-topped hill. Beneath them spread a vast meadow, acres long, miles wide, full of blue and red and yellow flowers of the daisy family. Blue swallowtail and white miniature butterflies flitted from flower to flower, imbibing nectar through their uncoiled probosci. Off in the distance, the chlorophyll wall of the interior loomed like a horizon-wide barrier of greenery—a three-tiered fortress of flora. Chelsea's characteristically stern lips melted into a smile. The man was clearly in his element.

Work began immediately, Giles and Chelsea chasing butterflies with the vigor and enthusiasm of school children as the porters set up camp. The soldiers, a dozen strong, rested on their weapons, laughing at the two white men's prancing among the fields. They would have stories to share when they returned to the barracks, bar room tales of the professor goose-stepping through the flowers, of his dandy young companion's glee and gloating at catching a simple insect.

Dusk inked the sky purple as the two collectors entered their tent. Here they stacked their chloroform jars and jotted down notes in an observation journal. Giles made some preliminary sketches of the more unusual wing shapes. They were hopelessly mechanical and altogether too crude to convey any sense of organic substance. He may as well have drawn an engineering diagram of a steam engine as try to catch the subtle flutterings of a swallowtail as it skitted across the grass.

"Chadwick!"

"What is this refuse?"

"If only you could...capture life."

The stabbing pain in his neck, which had been absent while collecting samples, returned. Dry lightning shot off in the distance, setting up a sympathetic reaction with the throb as if the crackling plasma exacerbated the sting with its barely felt shock waves. It would be a long night. Sleep came fitfully in cascading waves of increasing fever. Giles felt nauseous from the hemorrhaging stream of stings so near the base of his skull. The lightning and thunder drew nearer, pulsing rapid-fire in and out of his brain.

"Bwana. Something is near our camp." Giles woke to the soldier's voice. Chelsea barely responded to the guard's insistent prodding. "The men are worried for fear of demons or sorcerers."

"They'll see a demon if this is a false alarm," Chelsea retorted groggily. Lightning now flashed near the hilltop camp. Giles noted that through the whole night of approaching lightning, not a drop of rain had fallen. Not even a breeze blew in let alone the cool winds that normally portend a thunderstorm. A strange storm to shower no rain in monsoon season.

He followed Chelsea and the soldier out of the tent, then turned back to retrieve his forgotten pith helmet.

The air exploded.

Giles flew into the canvas tent wall, wrapped up in its thick fabric as glass, wood and dirt showered over him. He heard the snapping crackle of electricity, but was so bound by the tent cloth that he could not break free to see what damage had been done by the lightning blast.

Gunfire erupted from the camp's perimeter. Shouts swept across the hilltop, bouncing through the unwanted turban that engulfed Giles' head and face like a mummified python.

"Njoni hapa! Upesi, upesi!"

"Hapana! Tunaenda Nyumbani," followed by several bodies running past, some stepping on the tent remains that still pinned him tight.

More gunfire, two or three shots from an electroshock rifle, then shouts.

"Hapana! Nzi mkubwa! Tuko hapa, tuko hapa!"

Frantic screams, no words now, only terror—erupted from behind him as he finally extricated himself from the remaining tent shreds. His neck flamed in agony, dropping him to his knees. He was barely able to crane his head up to see what was happening.

The camp lay strewn with charred bodies, smoking in the dull glow of innumerable small fires. Only a handful of soldiers remained, the rest of the camp either fled or slain. Before them loomed two gargantuan, silver-chested apes, tree-high with four arms flailing from each torso. The troops stabbed with their bayonets, piercing each giant with their steel slivers. It looked as if they would gain the advantage over the mutant simians as the giants visibly slowed under the blades' onslaught.

Then a whir, an electric whine spun up from just outside the camp, to Giles' right. Sparkles flickered around a long tubular projection as the whine increased in frequency and intensity. Behind the tube, atop the vehicle to which it was affixed, sat two dark figures aiming the device at the battling guards.

This Kabilar had a lightning gun. A lightning gun!

Light flooded the camp as the sky cracked open, a forked stream of electricity catching the remaining soldiers mid-rib, thrusting their tattered remains tumbling a hundred feet or more into a smoking heap down the hillside, a trail of sparks tracking back across the electrified earth to the artillery piece.

The dark impressions of the gunners had etched themselves onto Giles' retinae as the hell fire passed. Both figures were naked; one with the lower torso of a striped tsetse, the upper torso of a native woman; the other with four arms that ended not in hands, but in insectoid claws. Giles lay flat for fear of being discovered.

The Kabilars ransacked the camp, genetically obscene mixtures of insect and human DNA picking through the bodies, eating raw flesh and dancing amid the smoldering corpses. One winged child held Chelsea's singed and severed head aloft and threw it to passing feasters at the banquet of dead flesh. They promptly chewed Chelsea's eyeballs out of their sockets. Screeches and laughter flooded the night air, a bacchanalian racket that frightened birds and monkeys from the distant trees. The gorilla mutants beat their chests in spite of their wounds, their bellows trailing off into the valley to join the echoes of the Kabilar's din.

A click and the touch of cold steel on the neck flooded Giles' body numb with fear. His spine burned as if a red-hot rivet had been driven in—but no shot had been fired. The shotgun barrel simply hovered there above his neck. He ventured movement, fully aware that he should be dead already.

The gamble paid off in a clear view of his would-be executor. Long, pale legs led up to a naked torso, female, athletic. His eyes traced copper hair up from the shoulders, exquisite ropes of cellulose that ended in the head of Emile Beckwith.

Her eyes were without white or color—pure black. Only with the few remaining flickers of firelight was he able to see that her eyes were not smooth, but shone with a hundred facets in the burning glow. He suppressed his nausea but was still unable to speak.

She whispered to the injured Giles "play dead"—the slightest hint of a buzz to her words—then struck his head sharply with the gun's butt. The last thing he saw as he swooned was a flying form, half-tsetse, half-infant, above Emile, in the air. The Great Fly had found him again.

Red, sunburned skin scratched his nerve endings to consciousness. Cracks must be appearing inside his throat, he thought. With great effort he strained to raise himself up on his elbows. The hillside fluttered black and white in the afternoon sun—the corpse-infested ground covered with a snow fall of *Papilio Odius*. A million death heads winked at him from the carrion heaps, skulls flying from skull to skull, a cool winged breeze counteracted by the rising heat of fermenting bodies. Here were enough specimens to make him wealthy forever, but never enough to buy back his sanity or return his obliterated longing for the fly-sympathizer—or was it fly-lover, for the child-thing was white—

Emile Beckwith, not enough to return his innocence. He traced the impression of a female footprint left in the loamy soil. Their trail led west, toward the interior.

He reached back to massage his neck: A black antenna grew out from the center of the bump. The fly was now a part of him. The burning pain had stopped.

Coda

Iglensk and Dutarov sat leaning against the outside wall of the elephant pit. They smoked unfiltered cigarettes and shared lewd jokes, as hired guards often do. There was not much else to do as security officers of the Kinderzeit zoo. Smoke, joke and talk.

"So this new elephant keeper. I hear he's crazy."

"Who here isn't?" Dutarov quipped.

"No, certifiably bonkers."

"Really?"

Iglensk took a long drag off his cigarette, exhaling words with his carcinogens. "Government shipped him in after a court appearance. Seems he killed a white man down in the tropics, then wiped out the porters and guards who had gone along on the expedition."

"How could he do it alone?"

"Who knows? The air down there does strange things to a man."

"I know," agreed Dutarov. "One of the guys I trained in the army went down there. The most innocent boy you know, a mama's boy. The army didn't even soil his spirit. He went down south, though, and came back with the clap and a bounty on his head."

"Yes, there seems to be no end to the evil churned up in that humid air. Anyway, as I was saying, he killed the whole lot of them, then burned their bodies. It appears that some of them may have been cannibalized."

"Cannibalized? Don't tell me—dismissed on grounds of insanity."

"Yes. Then the judge sent him here to work with the animals. Since the chap had worked here before, the judge reasons, the return to life as it was before he went to Ngome might serve to restore a bit of his mental health."

"Do you think there really is a cure for such a person?"

"I don't know. He seems tranquil enough, though. Doesn't cause any problems. You would think..."

An alarm klaxon stopped Iglensk in mid-sentence. They both sprang to their feet, looking for the source of the disturbance.

A shadow fell over them and melted southward.

Above them floated a large gray mass. An elephant calf, dead, trunk, tail and limbs hanging limp toward the ground like a jellyfish's tentacles. The pachyderm glided smoothly through the air. The guards blinked, dropping their rifles, and it was several seconds before the shock left them enough vision to glimpse colors splashing along the calf's topside. Ten thousand butterflies, each attached to the rough skin by a metal needle, carried the body aloft over the zoo walls.

Chadwick Giles sat cross-legged in the elephant pen, a half-spilled jar of pins at his side. He watched the dead animal's ascension with great interest—through his multi-faceted, blackened eyes. The winds that tickled his antenna would, he knew, eventually take the beast's corpse back to its homeland, near Ngome. He understood now what it meant to bring his art to life.

The Nut Lady's Cabin

In a northern town there sat a house on the banks of the mighty Mississippi. Travelers came from time to time to see the flower-covered hillside around the little log cabin. In the early morning one could see an old lady, name unknown, age unrevealed—though well beyond the lasciviousness of youth and the bittersweet age of childbearing—step through the door and throw out nuts for the waiting squirrels. Gray, time-worn eyes, set like flawed jewels in her thin face, lent an air of wisdom to the body beneath her silver mop of hair.

The rodents seemed well acquainted with the old lady, approaching fearlessly as she stooped to take them up in her arthritic arms and let them climb up on her shoulders and back—tame and affectionate as housecats. They would eat nuts right from her hand, though they never approached other humans, keeping distance from all passers-by, preferring to keep company only with their benefactor. The elderly caregiver also avoided contact with others of her species, viewing them as evil, sensuous, uncaring, sinful. She would rather consecrate her time to the noble pursuit of caring for her "little ones," as she so tenderly called them, viewing them as cherubic children—children in need of protection from the cruelty of the human race.

Spring and Summer came and went, then one Autumn day the cold came early, wilting the flowers with injections of frost. The old lady fed the unusually large crowd of squirrels, letting them frolic about her skirt and blouse as was their habit. One black squirrel climbed onto her head, becoming entangled in her hair and it was only with much effort that she freed it from her gray strands. She set it gently on the ground then went back into the house to get more nuts—the group of squirrels had grown substantially larger.

All at once, the pack was on the cabin, clambering up the sides, gnawing through the window panes and door, clogging the chimney flue with their asphyxiated, convulsing carcasses. Claws clattered along the walls and roof while the house became encrusted with fur, streams of bushy-tailed squirrels flowing from the surrounding woods to converge on the little log cabin, raping its crevasses with their engorged mass.

A stuttering protest, screams constricted by senescence, chittered from between the old woman's parched lips. But the horde was relentless in its conquest, nipping and scratching her frailness into submission, forcing her to squat down on the pile of acorns beneath her brittle hips as they bored through her body tissue like living phallic drills.

The sky darkened and snow fell, slowly at first, then in gusts of sticky blobs. The rodent horde continued to snake in and out of the house, furry tendrils infiltrating the dwelling, making it a living, breathing structure, then a pulsing pile of snow and finally—at the height of the blizzard—a nondescript hump on the riverside landscape.

Spring came and melted the winter whiteness, except for a high snow mound in the midst of the bright pink, yellow and blue flowers. It wasn't until June that winter released the quiet cabin and revealed a mighty oak growing through the roof. The snow melted, but shards and slivers of glistening white could still be seen—there, entwined in the budding branches, arms cruciform, hung a gleaming skeleton, an empty jar of nuts clasped in one hand. The trunk of the tree thrust up through the pelvic opening and out through the ribs, violating the old lady's remains with impregnation and transforming her erst-while frame into a perverse shrine to the fertility goddesses of eons past. A lone black squirrel skittered off the skull's temple, down the trunk and out of the house, then scurried into the glowing green woods beyond the flower fields.

The Bones of Ndundi:
An Archaeology

Time is measured here by physical need. Asking "when is mealtime?" gets you an incredulous stare and: "Whenever you are hungry"; "When is bed time?"—an exasperated sigh and "When you are tired." This does not, of course, betray any kind of "savage innocence," as the colonial officials of the past would have called it—time *is* largely irrelevant in the camps. All things are provided: shelter, food, water, medical aid—though not at the same comfort level to which Westerners are accustomed. With these needs met, what need does one have for "last week" or "next month" or "at three o'clock"? Time as measured by watches and calendars is an indistinct smear in this part of Africa.

Eras, however, are not a foreign concept, imported from across the seas and imposed by governmental edict. Our mid-twentieth century is referred to as "The Time Before the Big Troubles"—not because "big troubles" (a euphemism for ethnic cleansing) were unknown, but because the space between these culturally traumatic events during that period was much greater than it is today.

I once asked an elder to tell me about the time before Nyanya Baruki bore children; when she and the elders were young. "Oh! That is ancient history—when the colonials were in charge." The twenty years before the refugees fled to this camp was a cacophony of fear and blood sprinkled with short pauses of uneasy, near-paranoid "peace." People refer to the era in which we now live as "The Time of Sadness."

As events unfold these eras compress and expand in the minds of past participants like some chronological accordion, speeding up and slowing down the historical tempo. These fluctuations of collective memory cannot be caught on paper. Paper records are unknown among camp dwellers. Only the military keeps such records—or outsiders, such as I.

I am the nexus of catalogue and internal reflection. Two journals cover my desk: the thin, jittery hand of my personal diary—loose sheaves, tickets, knick knacks and souvenirs spilling from the pages; and the official tribunal evidence record: sharp, neat records painstakingly typed in a uniform font on a device entirely too modern for such a remote rural piece of Africa.

I knew the bones animate, speaking, laughing, drunk and playing. The catalogue knows numbers, diagnoses, the marks of evidence.

Rarely do the two works cite one another.

Sample NR201a:

Large pitting of female os coxae indicates possible ante-mortem parturition, though the weak correlation between pitting and pregnancy leave a large margin for diagnostic error.

Nyanya Baruki is not, despite the Swahili title "nyanya," a grandmother at all. While she had children of her own, the line seems to have been cursed with barren-ness. This curse, as it appears to some, combined with widow Baruki's methuselanic age, has done much to spawn rumors of sorcery and black magic around her person. Pregnant women dutifully avoid her gaze, fearful of spontaneous abortion. Even those who distribute food from the rice trucks hand her portion to her next of kin to avoid any possibility of contamination by evil spirits.

I once interviewed Mzee Mangome about her youth:

"Her father was a carpenter?"

"Yes. Ndwele Baruki made the best plows for many villages around. He would take a cart full to market each week and come back jingling with money—real money, like the kind you could pay taxes with back then."

"And her mother?"

"Grew tomatoes as big as your clenched hands. She also sold at market. Between the two of them, they were a rich family indeed."

"What of her education?"

"Well, the Belgians only let her take four years of grammar, but she was very good at it. Of course the elders at the time were furious at her, though they could not express their anger around the missionaries. When the fathers weren't looking, though, they would give her a good scolding, if not a beating for her cheekiness."

"What did she do after her schooling came to an end?"

"Raised goats, like everyone else her age."

"Goats?"

"They did not own cattle. They were no Tutsis."

"And after that?"

"A young man from Butare, who was passing through trading goats at the time, became enamored of her. He gave half his flock to make the young woman his bride."

"And he stayed in the village?"

"He traveled frequently to do his trading. She bore him four children before he died."

"What happened?"

"He drowned trying to cross the Rusizi to Bukavu. The news took a few days to reach the village, but when it came it spread silence across her face, like her soul had left for the dark of the forest."

"I'm sorry. It must have been devastating. And what of her children?"

Fugue XXIX

"They grew old and have married. But that is part of another time."

Through this and several other conversations with Mzee Mangome, I never heard any hint of condescension, no evil speaking behind Baruki's back. I thought that perhaps his non-judgmental attitude was simply a mark of respect born out of shared experience—both had seen the schismatic transition from colonial to post-colonial rule at a young age. Those of the next generation had grown up under black rule their entire lives.

Only later did I understand the dichotomy of attitudes regarding Nyanya Baruki. An over-zealous young woman, a Christian girl, newly baptized, came to me in a state of great alarm, warning me that a group of women were about to administer "the old rituals" to some young women who had recently reached puberty. I knew what the old rituals entailed, and was concerned from a wholly sanitary viewpoint—religious disagreements were not my concern, nor was it my purview to interfere in this regard.

I gathered my bag and headed for the forest, running behind the young zealot. Muffled screams greeted me as I rounded a thicket and walked into a grove just as Nyanya Baruki exited the hut, clitorodectomy stone in hand, the blood of pubescence covering her arms and hands. From the hands of the grandchild-less—a new group of mothers-to-be. Fruit from the barren hands, a blessing from the cursed.

Sample NR19b,c,d

Cranial metric methods for establishing geophysical ancestry are fraught with difficulty, though several such procedures exist. The large skull fragments of individual 19 were tested against both Howells' and Gill's criteria in this instance because of the abundance of comparative material and because the remains of individual 19 were identified by locals as that of a prominent moderate Tutsi allegedly killed by other, more radical Tutsi soldiers during the massacre of Ndundi Hutu... indeed, the cranial metric methods employed reveal that the remains of individual 19 are morphologically indistinct from those of other individuals in the study sample.

Peter Banyuro came to me on a stretcher. He had been badly wounded while interfering with a Zairean soldier who had taken a fancy to one of the local girls. Banyuro's delicate cheek was swollen purple, bruised from shattered flecks of orbitale and ectoconchon that had been buried in the muscle

"He caught the soldier with his pants down," one of my attendants told me. "But the soldier's caught prying Peter with his rifle butt, even with his ankles all tied up!" Banyuro laughed at the comment, then winced in pain, smiled, then groaned. His agonized frivolity was not lost on my attendant, who pulled faces and cracked jokes in an effort (I hoped) to distract the suffering man from his wounds.

"Peter, you should have knocked! Then he would not have knocked you!"

and

"You must tell me, was it the rear guard or just the guard's rear? It's good for you he didn't make a frontal assault!"

I shushed them and asked my attendant to hold Banyuro's head still while I made some incisions. The bone was close to the skin and I wanted to remove some of the splinters to prevent festering and infection. I sliced his smooth cheek as delicately as possible, crimson pouring over the scalpel blade and handle, dripping to the table, and removed as much of the damaged bone as I felt I ought to, Banyuro smiling all the while.

The cheerful gleam suddenly left his eye, though, as someone entered the room behind me. I was too busy applying pressure and gauze to note who had walked into my office uninvited. I expected to look up to the barrel of an AK-47. I raised my eyes to my attendant, his dread-washed expression sending cold shivers down my back, then turned to see Banyuro's Hutu wife standing there in the doorway. Her narrow eyes revealed displeasure.

"Misses Banyuro. Come in."

She looked through me at her husband. Peter Banyuro wore a grave face, frightened, but dignified.

"Carousing again, Peter?" Ice.

"Misses Banyuro," my attendant defended the patient. "Mister Banyuro was defending the honor of a young woman when he was viciously set upon by a group of Zairean Askari!"

She looked decidedly unconvinced, resolute in her conviction that it was all a lie, hands on hips, pursed lips and head bobbing side to side: "Mm-hmm?" I averted my gaze, a feeling of embarrassment pulsing in my chest, like a child who must watch his friend being reproached by his mother in public.

"My wife," Banyuro spoke seriously for the first time since he was carried in to my office. "Go home. I will be with you after the doctor has bandaged my wounds."

Then silence. Long silence.

The sighs that simultaneously hissed from the men's mouths signaled the OK to speak freely. The woman was gone. Banyuro was sitting up now, and spoke first.

"Thank you, my doctor," then, turning to my attendant, "my friend."

They smiled at one another.

"Peter," my attendant laughed, "maybe you should try your luck again with the soldier!"

And Peter Banyuro once again recoiled in pain, holding his hand to his bandaged, mangled face, laughing in agony.

SampleNR34g,h

Tibia exhibit significant morphological divergence from other bones in the sample study. These bones are clearly shorter than the sample's adult average and are more dense. Cut marks to malleolar groove and soleal line might be indicative of cannibalism, though lack of intentional fracturing and signs of burning make this assessment unlikely.

Bernault was the laughing stock of the camp, though he hardly knew it. Like any good participant-observer the journalist-turned-aid worker did his best to live as the locals, to "go Fante" as the British used to say. Unfortunately, Bernault misunderstood the dynamics of loyalty, mistaking empathy—in the Western sense of feeling the pain of others by suffering as they suffer—for dedication, for fondness, for brotherhood.

His sacrifices went deeper than condescension, though the elders would still ridicule him: "There is no news here," they would tell him, "and you are lucky the soldiers only stole one of your cameras!" He would smile back, wanting to believe that their comments were in good-humor. They were not. Their smiles were confused—fed by a hope that if one smiles long enough, problems sort themselves out. Why would he, a wealthy (by their standards) European, choose to spend his time and health feeding and filming a few hundred Rwandan refugees? Why did he eat rice when he could afford meat? What was the purpose of asking questions, of taking photographs, of a ragged group of landless farmers and goat herders? Was the Frenchman making money from this venture? Was the aid-worker's uniform all a guise? Confusion and questions. This is what the West brought.

By the time I took him in, Bernault (he preferred to be called by his last name) was deteriorating quickly. His already thin frame was beginning to appear etiolated, as if he were one of the refugees whose plight he so desperately wished to document. His eyes were languid, but I could not be sure if this listlessness came as a symptom of starvation or of willful naïveté. At the least, his lack of energy belied the habit of eating only high-fat foods—he was getting enough calories, as did all in the camp, but to show satisfaction at mealtime would mean a betrayal of his martyrdom.

Nevertheless, I fed him. My maid, Buranda, was an outstanding cook, trained at a restaurant in Kampala that fed wealthy Europeans who had "lost their way," they would tell her, on safari from Tanzania. Buranda's sense of propriety forbade her from asking where these wayward rich were going—and from whom they were fleeing. Instead, she would offer a special discount to these renegades: "You give me a recipe, I give you free drinks." Her offer was never turned down. Alcohol lubricated the road from the past, speeding the banished to their destination: anonymity.

Buranda saw in Bernault a young man in flight. "No, not from the law, not from criminals," she would tell me as he slept on a cot on the veranda. "He is trying to escape his family. He feels bad that his family has so much money. Guilty. He looks for secrets here to escape his own."

"But you can't fault him for feeling this way," I replied. "Nor for acting it. If he wants to starve himself for some higher good, can you blame him? It's not the most intelligent act, but perhaps it feeds his soul in some meaningful way."

"No!" she responded sharply. "No! It burns his soul."

"How so?"

"Doctor, you live in the biggest house for miles around."

"Yes," I replied, confused.

"Why? There is only one of you."

I thought. "I suppose so that people can find me."

"Exactly. Because when they need help, they know where to go."

"And?" still confused.

"You don't hide your talent as a doctor, you show the world: 'Here is Doctor Matthew's house—come here if you are sick'. People know that if they need help they can come to you to get better."

She shook her head at my uncomprehending look. "This Frenchman—he has money. How do you think he got through the border with his camera? You know how the guards 'tax' everyone who comes through." I was all too aware of the practice—some of the worst fractures I had seen came as a result of a failure to pay 'tax'. "So why doesn't he show us that he is rich? He could really help some of us. Instead he buries his money and his past—like it is dirty. He is a liar, Doctor. He lies to himself and to us. This is why I say he is burning his soul."

At breakfast the next morning, Bernault hesitantly ate his food— sausage, eggs and milk—in the cook's presence. He leaned over his plate, mouth thick with sausages and a thick French accent: "Doctor. Thank you for the food. Maybe I'm not suited to eating like the natives, but I must. I must persist. It's the only way I can learn their secret history. I must know who here is hiding—who here fears for justice for the murders they might have committed. I have my suspicions, Doctor."

Buranda took off her apron, then, leaning on the table, spoke as a mother chiding her child: "Je vais vous dire quelque chose, homme Français: il n'y a pas d'assassins parmis nous. Voila notre secret—celui que vous cherchez depuis si longtemps. Il n'y a pas de secret."

Fugue XXIX

We both sat, two dumbfounded Europeans, stunned by her fluent French. The camp might not have its secrets, but Buranda clearly had hers.

SampleNR18j, p

Posterior right scapula shows severe abrasion of acromion process passing mediolaterally to scapular spine. The gleno-humeral joint between scapula and humerus shows a comminuted fracture without callus, indicating peri- or post-mortem damage. Comminuted fractures to the occipital, wormian bone and asterion, with associated abrasion, indicate repeated trauma to the back of the head.

"Oppression!"

The many-voiced cry emanating from the church woke me in the night. Soon after, an insistent rapping at my door drew me from bed. A voice greeted me, sounding distant and muffled to my groggy ears.

"Doctor, you must come to the church. Mzee Mangome clutches his chest!"

I bolted for the church, the glow from within a beacon to my crusted eyes. By the time I had reached the doors the cold had fully awakened me.

Inside, two masses opposed one another. To my left, a small group of young, lithe boys, mostly teenagers, stood pointing and shouting at those on my right: the camp elders, most sitting with calm, measured expressions, save those few who were assisting Mzee Mangome, who lay curled on the floor in obvious agony off to one corner. Both groups briefly turned to watch me walk in, then promptly ignored me as I tended to the fallen elder. I was a necessary hindrance to their talks.

Debate raged around and over me. It was useless to ask for silence, so I set about my diagnoses as best I could under the cacophony. Perhaps my own endorphins allow me to recall a debate that was so peripheral to my task at hand. My senses were heightened by the knowledge that Mangome might well be having a heart attack. I worked with one soul, listened with another. Two people of the same body.

"You are holding us back. You have heard what they say on the radio."

Look for signs of chest pain.

"The radio is full of rumor."

Check breathing.

"But the army is advancing south."

Scan eyes.

"There have been no confirmed killings. We will allow them to pass through peacefully. Their business lies deep in Zaire, not here at the border."

Take pulse.

"But the blue helmets have pulled out. There is no one left to protect us. We must strike before we are stricken. We are ready—let us fight."

Left arm blue.

"Such fighting is exactly what got us here. We might not have lost our lands, our jobs, if we had restrained the extreme elements among us."

Remove constricting robes.

"No person is an element. You are old enough to remember how the colonials favored the Tutsi, treated us like dirt—like an element."

Pulse dropping.

"Yes, we are old. And we remember a time of peace."

Breathing shallow.

"A time of oppression."

Eyes unresponsive. No reaction to light.

"Wages or life? Which do you want? I prefer life, peace."

No pulse.

"To live without liberty is death! Better that we die trying."

Breathing stopped.

"You may say so, but you do not speak for the community. We, the elders, speak for the community. If you choose to fight and die when you lead, so be it. We will not allow it. We declare for peace."

The shouting continues, a cloud of killer bees inside my numb head.

The old one is dead.

One less voice fuels the debate.

The fervor of argument bounces off the church walls, vibrating through my bones.

But I hear nothing.

A young man's mouth opens, closes, spits in slow motion, yelling at the remaining elders. I see it as a disembodied instrument, floating free of the face to which I know it must be attached, a machine. There are not words. No words. Words. No.

Video:

Black to static to white, bleeding slowly to full color.

A view down a muddy village street, makeshift huts to either side.

A horde of men brandishing machetes and firing rifles into the air cross the bridge leading into the village.

A low roar of shouts, vehicles in the distance, then silence as the camera's sound shuts off.

Inhabitant's scatter for the woods, a large group of women and children—some elderly men—head for the small cement-block church.

From left a group of young men—about ten strong—rushes toward the oncoming group waving machetes.

Uniformed soldiers ooze out from the crowd, take aim at the charging youth, shoot low, for the legs. Bodies fall.

The onrushing horde threads out, filters the village's creases, greases the walls with blood.

A black hand reaches toward the camera lens.

Whirlwind blur, the world in vertigo.

A European man, on his knees, in the middle of the street, camera attachments on his back and belt.

Two men stretch his arms out, two his legs, as a fifth machete hacks off his hands and feet.

Pan up to a jeep driving past at high speed, one of the brave young machete-wielding defenders of the village chained by his ankle to the back bumper, his head and shoulders repeatedly bouncing on the road. Sound comes back as the engine dopplers into the distance.

Follow the jeep, pan left to the church where soldiers throw hand-grenades through the open windows. Sound lost again in multiple explosions. Doors blown off.

Pan right: a man holds a bloodied machete in one hand, a human head in the other, high above his head, smiling.

Ghosts crawl over my bones, beneath my skin. My pelvis aches from childbirth. My mandible is sore from debate. My hand is permanently curled in the shape of a camera handle. My cheek is shattered from a Zairean rifle-butt blow.

I am to be introduced to the court as a witness. "What did you see?" they will ask. I will remain silent. "Where were you at the time of the attack?" And I will not answer. "Why do you not answer the question?" I will tell them: "When do you eat? When you are hungry. Sleep? When you are tired. Respond to questions? When you have answers. I have no answers."

Time ends when all your friends are gone. It is a new era. The time of silence.

Beyond the Flame

Look above and beyond the flame and you will see features in the background bubble and bulge, shrink and retreat, like the reflections of one running back and forth through a hall of funhouse mirrors. Such was the effect when S/he, man-queen and woman-king of the desert, walked through the recently breached wall of The Porcelain City. S/he's gas-masked, flamethrower-wielding minions laid waste to the whitewashed buildings that lined the marble-cobblestone streets, cackles erupting from under their red-hooded cowls as they sprayed napalm on the inhabitants of that once-great metropolis. They poured through the catapult-broken fortification like streams of flaming blood, penetrating every street and alley, rooster-tails of smoke flying up in their wake.

S/he stepped over the smashed remains of those buildings unfortunate enough to have been built nearest the wall on which S/he's army's spearhead had thrust. S/he was an astounding figure: A full black beard under curly black hair; full lips smeared with bright red lipstick and gloss, bright blue eye shadow contrasting with deep-set brown eyes under a strong protruding, almost Neanderthal, brow. In all, you might say S/he's face was a disaster. S/he's body was even more deliciously hideous. The chest was clearly female, but for the hair that erupted from under a red-and-black lace brassiere like an explosion of curled black fur. The belly was long, a touch plump (though by no means obese) and equally hirsute. Arms and legs were brawny and thick, while the thong-covered groin was...indeterminate.

The heat waves generated by burning structures and burning

corpses reflected off the bleached walls of The Porcelain City, shrinking and growing S/he's features so that S/he alternately looked like a muscle-bound weightlifter, a petite (yet thickly-bearded) vixen, and any number of varied mutants, lepers, and sufferers of a hundred different forms of elephantitis that the cosmos saw fit to inflict on mankind.

Strangely, these same heat waves did not seem to affect S/he's pet, which was held fast on a thin black leather leash. The pet always looked like, and always was, a Scarlet Ibis, that beautiful and mystic bird of the Nile.

The ibis spoke first.

"You seek wisdom in The Porcelain City, yet your minions burn to embers those that might give it. Sparks and flame only speak cleansing and death, not wisdom."

S/he responded in a soprano falsetto, altogether too high for the bulk of that body. "S/he hungers for wisdom," then yelling in tin-whistle-third-octave pitch: "Stop the fires!"

A chorus of deep male voices echoed down the line. "Stop the fires! Stop the fires!"

Soon, steam billowed up from every district, and the troops were horrified to see that S/he was even more hideous without the transforming effects of heat and flickering flame.

The soldiers, now bored and waiting for orders, watched closely as their junior commander, General Clock Eyes, approached S/he, walking back from the central command post, which had already been established in the city's charred heart, to debrief his senior. Clock Eyes was ceremonious, as one would expect from a veteran general. His skeletal hand snapped up in salute to his shining white frontal lobes, shading his pocket-watch eyes, which read two-o'clock and twenty after seven, respectively. The timing gave him a touch of lazy-eye, but he was no dullard. He had snuck into the city—one can imagine the ease with which a skeleton might skulk into a completely porcelain city unseen— and cut power to the defending residents, shattering their resolve to keep the attacking army at bay. After that, it was only a matter of time before the naked General's men would take the city.

But now he had clothed himself in a dark gray ascot and neon green cravat, a gaudy, though bold leader of men, showing a hint of thigh bone and patella between the hem of his tartan plaid kilt and high woolen socks. His nailed boots clacked as he dropped his salute.

"Supreme Commander," he barked from an unseen larynx, words traveling over an unseen tongue. "We have captured the Burgermeister of The Porcelain City."

"Excellent," the ibis said, S/he too busy looking around at the steam-filled streets to listen to General Clock Eye's report. The bird continued, "We will see him at once!"

Clock Eyes led the pair through the thin, winding streets of that ancient city, past smoldering refuse, half-collapsed buildings that had spilled their furnishings and once-living inhabitants onto the once-white sidewalks, now veined in red and black. They walked along a mile-long convoy of overturned rickshaws laying in splinters beside the main thoroughfare leading to the religious quarter.

The rickshaw road opened suddenly onto an immense oval courtyard flanked by fully two dozen high minarets, each topped by pear-shaped watchtowers through which was piped a cacophony of ululating prayers—outcries, really, against whatever gods had abandoned the city in its hour of greatest need.

S/he craned eyes upward to the sky, back cracking and vertigo-induced from the height of it all.

But Ibis's gaze was fixed on the bumpy dome that dominated the courtyard. It squatted there like a giant turtle riven with a network of irregular cysts atop its shell, each cyst a dome-atop-a-dome with tiny windows circling its circumference. The metal skin of the building had rusted into a thick crust that mimicked Ibis's plumage in color.

The steam and smoke of the morning's assault was thrown to tatters by a southerly wind, and soon the sun beat down on the courtyard. Heat waves emanated from the white marble cobblestones, their distorting flux giving the dome the appearance of a pulsing red heart as noon ascended. A pair of guards, hidden from the heat by a circular doorway, spun a metal wheel and opened the dome's ship-portal door to let the trio enter.

S/he squealed in discomfort as S/he's eyes adjusted to the sudden darkness. The inside of the dome was painted flat black, and several thin beams of sunlight that shot through the upper windows a hundred feet above provided the only light within.

The Burgermeister greeted them with a smile and outstretched forelimbs, a long, thin sword-cane dangling from his wrist. The friendly grin was not without pain. Two of the tank-sized spider's lesser eyes had been gouged out, and his seventh leg was gimpy from some injury, though neither S/he nor Ibis could identify the true problem in the dimness. A few dead soldiers wrapped up in webbing near the roof, along with the blood smearing his cane, gave proof that the Burgermeister had not submitted without a fight.

He tipped his immense top hat, chitin scraping beneath his tuxedo as he bowed his pencil-mustached and sharply-bearded face to the floor. He spoke in a deep, rich voice, full of poise and charisma, as befitted one of his standing.

"Greetings, esteemed visitors of The Porcelain City. How may I be," a pause, then, "your humble servant?"

"You do well to grovel," Ibis stated flatly, his beak held high in a stance that belied a touch of haughtiness. "Your once-bright city lies in ruins and your fair citizens are ravaged by our unstoppable army."

"You flatter me with your compliments, Ibis. I am truly not worthy of your generosity."

Ibis's features softened. He gave a respectful nod to the Burgermeister, who turned his thorax to the three and began moving to the far side of the dome. He spoke to them over his shoulder.

"Come. The document is being prepared. We will discuss the terms of my surrender. The advantage will, of course, be yours, though I am sure you will find the terms satisfactory as they stand."

S/he spoke out while following the gigantic spider. "I seek wisdom."

The spider stopped suddenly and turned toward S/he, the smile fading from his face. His two main eyes squinted as if he were trying to peer in and understand S/he's motives.

"Wisdom?" The Burgermeister's voice was full of incredulity. "Wisdom is elusive in these parts, and most rare, prized above gold and the finest of finery." But a smile soon creased his plump face again. "Of course, we will discuss this as a part of our negotiations."

He turned toward a small candle-lit table at the opposite end of the building, bowing and holding one arm extended, palm up. "Please, kind sirs, after you."

They passed the Burgermeister, and as they passed, his greasy smile sagged into a frown, then bloomed into a scowl as his legs tensed and his bulbous body shook with anticipation.

When it seemed he might burst from excitement, the crafty arachnid shot forth like a crossbow bolt, ramming the trio with his huge armored body. General Clock Eyes flew across the building and into the ceiling, fracturing into 208 distinct pieces—206 bones and two pocket-watch faces, both eternally showing XII o'clock. Ibis squawked, the leather leash whipping him into the air, then stop-snapping his neck at full length, scarlet feathers darting out into a cloud that floated lazily to the floor. S/he fell to knees, then came up throwing punches, great roundhouses that cleared the buxom chest too quickly for the spider to dodge as S/he's hairy knuckles hammered mayhem on the Burgermeister' face.

It cracked.

Simply cracked between the spider's two main eyes. The twelve-foot long spindly legs wobbled uncontrollably as ichor spilled out from the Burgermeister's head. Or was it oil? Yes! Oil—that came out in streams, polluted with tiny geared wheels, ball bearings, and wing nuts by the dozens. A great smoke issued out from under the spider's chitin, spewing from the seams in jets. A clunk, sputter, and whir later, the creature's legs gave out, and its body came down hard with an immense metallic clang that echoed off the dome walls, shaking flakes of rust down in a russet snow storm.

S/he stood staring at the hulk, fists at the ready. Ibis's leash had become caught around one of the Burgermeister's legs in the fray and now lay crushed beneath the weight of the spider-machine. General Clock Eyes was, of course, everywhere to be found, but nowhere at once, like some veiled and incomprehensible god.

But S/he ignored the bits of rust-dusted bone that littered the floor. Something else on the spider popped and the scraping sound of metal on metal preceded the appearance of a hatch opening in the top of the Burgermeister's head. The two halves of the mechanical arachnid's pate split apart, and from the fissure crawled another spider, identical to the first, complete with tuxedo, cane, and top-hat. But this creature was only the size of a man's fist. He saw S/he and cringed.

S/he's voice squeaked out: "Wisdom. I desire wisdom." S/he grabbed the Burgermeister's pilot (or was this the *real* Burgermeister?), pinching his walnut-sized head between thumb and forefinger. The Spider's top-hat tumbled to the floor as S/he lifted him up to eye level. "Give me my desire," and the squeak careened into a bass roar: "NOW!"

Fugue XXIX

Spider hung suspended, mandibles agape in shock, then collected himself with a shudder. He spoke very quickly, his voice the sound of a hundred spiders skittering across crystal.

"What wisdom I have, I give. If you would be wisest of all, remember these: hints, euphemisms, innuendo, insinuation, obfuscation, rumor, misdirection, subtleties, whispers, temptation, forestalling, false promises, misleadings, double speak, unfulfilled covenants..."

And S/he parted those immense ruby red lips and dropped the spider onto the pink carpet of tongue that filled S/he's maw, closing those huge yellow teeth in an inescapable prison.

The arachnid pressed and clawed for release—to no avail. S/he's forehead, cheeks, and eyes bubbled and bulged as the spider struggled to escape, protruding and collapsing, a boiling visage, like the reflections of one running back and forth through a hall of funhouse mirrors, or like shadows on a porcelain wall, beyond a flickering flame, filled with wisdom.

The Death Machines

You think Idi Amin Dada is dead, don't you? You read it in your Reuters, heard it on NPR, BBC, Radio Free Europe. Dead? No. The former Heavyweight Champeen is far from dead. You can rest easy that he is not resting in peace. No, far from it.

A new trinity rules hell on earth from an underground bunker in central Africa. Beelzebuth, Lucifer, and Ashtoreth have been superceded. Hastings Kamuzu Banda, the Minister of Misinformation, sits within the bone-built fortress, wires protruding from his head in a vast circuit array, which is, in turn, wired to a brisling clump of transceivers, microwave towers, and satellite dishes hidden within a volcanic crater in the nethermost reaches of what was once Zaire. His eyes are projectors, streaming two inch-thick optical cables worth of propaganda at high speed across the television sets of the world. Lies spew forth from his mouth into a microphone-mask that has been permanently welded to his jaw. You've heard whisperings of these lies as tiny packets of deception being bandied about from congressman to congressman, ambassador to ambassador, in dimly-lit coffee shops and bright board-walks, rich and poor firmly trapped in a vast, only partially-visible web. You will never know the whole of it. It would kill you if you heard it all, undiluted, at once. Dead. As dead as Idi Amin is not.

Banda does not act alone, however. He takes his orders from the Father of Farrago, Mobutu Sese Seko. Chaos is Mobutu's purview, and he approaches his duties with mathematical precision. You will never see Mobutu, though, even if you make it past the whited walls of that bone fortress buried deep within the African soil. You might, somehow, avoid the undead sentinels—an entire zombie army composed of past dictators and their most cruel minions—to the central room where he is located. But you would die of old age long before you were able to clamber, cut, and pull your way through the miles of circuits and wires that surround Mobutu. You see, he is entirely encased, buried alive in the machines that run the software that runs the algorithms that feed all the data necessary for the erstwhile despot to keep the world in that delicate balance between utter chaos (and, thus, utter freedom) and enough controlled chaos to instill a nagging uncertainty into the mind of every man, woman, and child on the planet. "Can I tell her?" "Is it safe?" "I'm not sure if I can trust you." Hence, Banda is the broadcaster, but Mobutu informs the content of the broadcast.

Back to Amin, now known as the Generalate of Hell's Armies. A government is only as strong as its enforcement. This is Idi Amin's forte. He had plenty of practice, back in the day. 250,000 dead under the auspice of the "Public Safety Unit"—the most ironically named internal police force in the history of mankind. Not bad for a little third world backwater like Uganda. Yes, the toll in Rwanda was likely twice that, but the Rwandan fire spread quickly, a flash in the pan, a wisp of smoke, then gone, all but ignored by most except the academics. The ghosts of Rwanda haunt graduate seminars and libraries, fearful of the machete-wielding campus gardener outside, come to chop ivy from the outside of the buildings. Amin's work was, and is, far more calculated than those amateurs' work. His task, to physically enforce Mobutu's calculations, requires the perfect touch: Not so much open violence to foment open rebellions, but enough back room brutality, combined with Banda's brilliant injections of doubt and mistrust, to keep things...interesting.

Despite all this decidedly modern machinery of mayhem, the

members of the trio have a romanticized notion of themselves. They see themselves as vulture-headed demons sitting in a candlelit scriptorium, the three of them surrounding a tall, circular table on which is etched a pentagram stained with blood. They hover, a hunched-over corvine wreath, stitching thaumatographies to parchment, composing threnodies and dirges from the screams of the tortured and dying with feathers plucked from the wings of the death angel herself.

But a new song emerges from outside the bone compound, a song of dark desires thrumming forth from the very dirt in which they calculate and commiserate. The notes of this song are new, written in an alphabet the Lords of Hell do not know:

gag-pol
env
tat
rev
nef
vif
vpr
vpu

The echoes are familiar to Mobutu, if not comprehensible, and he recalls a date and a place, though he knows not why: 1959. Kinshasa, Congo.

Banda repeats: "1959. Kinshasa, Congo." Mobutu is distraught, he did not wish this information to go out to the world. But Banda continues speaking what is, to his ears, gibberish: "CD4 protein is the main receptor on T-cells and macrophages...reverse transcription...integration...HIV..."

The machines malfunction. Mobutu's data has become garbled with feedback. His brain screams out in a high squeal as sparks flower up from his computerized coffin.

Amin, being the military man that he is, tries to hold it all together with brute force. But his troops have all gone soft on him. Uganda's Finest travel from village to village teaching about condoms and abstinence, but their efforts are in vain. And the Libyans and PLO, who fought alongside General Amin in those glory days of '78? Spineless apologists, as weak and helpless as his own soldiers. There is no help for the trio. The new song will seep through the very fossae of their bone fortress and, in time, take over as the new Ruler of Hell.

And the death machines roll around in their electronic graves, unable to sleep for the dreams of usurpation that crawl over their very circuits. Hell hath no end.

Improv and the Man of Means

Tony looked over her shoulder, past her diamond earring and golden hair, to the bandstand beyond. The musicians, stiff in starched white shirts (the antithesis of Brenda's jet dress, Tony noted) smiled with unmoving lips, their faces blank, eyes unblinking. Not an un-necessary muscle twitched—yet the fingers played on with precision, the trombones sliding in perfect synchronicity, each trumpet wail exact, violin bows stabbing the air in a military goose-stepping sameness.

Tony whisper-yelled above the music into Brenda's bejeweled ear: "This band—they're wonderful."

"You think so?" a worried expression formed over her face as he spun her down, then up, a fleshy dancing yo-yo.

"Yes, they don't miss a beat. Each one works like a piece of the same machine. They are obviously one in purpose—they even look alike. They make a fine big-band army, if you will."

Brenda could see them now over Tony's shoulder—blonde, slicked back hair meticulously plastered to each fine-featured head, identical pencil mustachios waxed to a point, instruments polished to sunshine brightness. They turned in lock-step to meet her gaze, all winking simultaneously at her, ice blue left eyes open-shut-open like pistons in a music machine. Their heads swiveled back to dead front straight-ahead, pursed smiles never slacking, continuing their mechanical play.

The torque of dance spun her vision around in a moil. Tony was a good dancer. Too good. She had been fumbling about all evening, apologizing for her clumsy feet. He had been a good sport thus far, uncomplaining. His style was stiff, but his execution was flawless, as if he moved on numbered feet with perfectly arched dashed lines between steps. It seemed he could not make a mistake.

His appearance was immaculate, from every fine hair on his head to the mirror polished dancing shoes on his nimble feet. His clean-shaven face smooth as the equine ice-sculptures rampant over the fruit bar in the back of the hall. Even his spotless white shirt, after long hours of dancing, was without wrinkle. He must have had it professionally pressed, Brenda thought, before he came to meet her—the well-manicured nails on his unblemished hands had obviously not been employed in menial tasks such as laundering. Here was a bachelor of $ome mean$. She was unaccustomed to men of mean$—and her best friend, Jane, had warned her about these types.

"They'll hook you in and let you go like a fish—catch and release, honey," a cloud of smoke spewed up from Jane's full lips, breaking into reverse-gravity rivers of tar and nicotine on her artificially red hair, adding texture to the already smoky pub.

"Better released than stuck with Mike," Brenda could feel tears coursing behind her eyes, waiting to flow out at the wrong word, the wrong memory trigger.

"Hon, he's over. Let that alone. That bastard was no good for anyone, especially such a sweetie like you."

"I'm trying to let him go, Jane, but you're not letting me."

"I just don't want to see you hurt, honey."

"I'll take my chances. With Mike gone..."

"Brenda, jail is not 'gone,' just temporarily removed from the picture."

"All right, with Mike removed I've got a new chance on life. I've been moved from cashier to book keeper, I'm in a more affordable place and making more money. It's time I move up a bit, Jane—and treat myself to a good man."

"A good man or the 'right' kind of man?" Jane flipped her fingers into quotation marks.

Brenda's silent non-response heightened the tension. Jane had to speak, lest the vacuum of words collapse in on their friendship: "Listen, I don't want to hurt you, but look at things. Before Mike you were as carefree a person as I've known. Nothing held you down, girl. You were bright, shining! 'Routine' was simply not a part of your vocabulary. You did what you wished and didn't care who you pissed off in the process."

A wry smile brushed across Brenda's face.

"And then you got involved with Mike."

The smile disappeared.

"That's when you gave yourself up."

"I thought he was fun, I..."

"He was fun. So fun that he took the fun right out of you, like some kind of vampire of good humor and charm. Brenda, he domesticated you."

Tears appeared again.

"That's why I'm worried about you. Maybe you have the money, the car, whatever—but the men you're eyeballing are looking for someone they can control, someone to tidy up while they're out golfing, someone to watch the kids while they make business contacts. They want a statuette, Brenda, and if you don't fit in their plush little box they throw you out."

The song ended and Tony began to lead Brenda to their booth.

"No," she insisted. "Stay out on the floor."

He shrugged and acquiesced, taking her hand in his as the band struck up the next song, fingers and arms all universal motion, like an orchestra of marionettes led by some unseen dictatorial puppet master.

Brenda dwelled on the comfortable anonymity of dancing, the ability to be invisible among a moving crowd, the music a veil behind which she could hide from herself.

    A discordant note caught her attention. Then another, and a string of syncopation and counterpoint. The serene wall of music, played by the mechanical band, was p-e-r-f-o-r-a-t-e-d by the shrill braying of a saxo-phone. From behind the bandstand a figure emerged, saxophone in hand. His notes flattened against the band's sharps, MAJORED against their minors and shrieeeeeked against their restzzz. A long mane of unkempt hair nearly hid his squinting green eyes from Brenda's view, but she could see his face: the effort, the concentration, the passion of his playing.

    Tony tried to speak to her, but the saxophonist's i

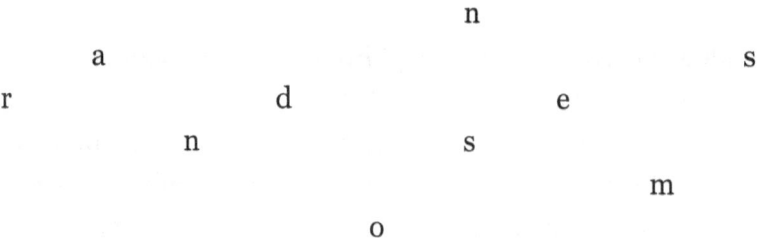

      R
                r
        E
                      g
          u
                        L
A
    r

    BLASTS interrupted his traintraintraintrain of thought: "The band can't...I wish he wouldn't...My feet can't...If only that instrument weren't so..." His steps faltered. Brenda saw in her mind a flurried mess of n1u2m3b4e5r6e7d footprints iSmUpPoEsRed in a chaotic

                  n
    a   s
r   d   e
      n   s
                      m
          o

—and his ankles buckled. Brenda could not suppress a laugh as he
F

   E

      L

         L

           to the floor, knocking a series of dancers > >>aside
and >>>>>>>>>>into>>>>>>>>>>   the band director.

The saxophone c|l|a|t|t|e|r|e|d on, intensifying the improvisation, stampeding over the sounds of the band, which continued to play its song as if the saxophonist were not present. They smiled and winked in unison at the dancers, ignoring the interruption.

Brenda offered her hand to Tony, but he was *oblivious.* A look of fear now creased his brow and one eye began to {t{t{w{w{i}t}t}c}h} uncontrollably. She laughed harder when he gripped the sides of his head as if to hold his skull plates together against entropy. His face contorted and thin cracks appeared on his cheeks and forehead. He screamed out and c-c-o-n-v-v-u-l-s-s-e-d-d on the floor, dark smoke seeping up through the seams as his face fell apart in clinking shards of porcelain that shattered and skidded across the shining wood to mingle with the eddying smoke and broken pieces of other dancers as they dis-

      -int-

         -eg-

           -r-

             -a-

               -t-

                 -e-

                    -d to the saxophone's wail.

Brenda bent double, drunken with laughter, then took the saxophonist's elbow in her hand. They walked toward the exit, her giggling

Fugue XXIX

and he smiling through pursed lips, the irregular shrieks of music and laughter puncturing [] air as []band popped fuses and shot jolts []electricity from [] decaying heads. [] chorus [] frogs [] crickets joined [] cacophony [] [] couple walked out [] door.

The Color of Laughter

No one told us *not* to go inside. The flashy e-literature we were force fed by the propaganda ministry was chock full of tourist-tempting positives—"Welcome to Ixchill 7," "A Cultural Guide to the K'kli," "Document 4315a: Official History of the K'kli"—but no restrictions on entering the structure, implied or otherwise, were to be found therein. Besides, we were bored military dependents whose parents had been assigned to a back water outpost of the Gaian Space Service. At least these were our excuses.

I was the new kid, fresh from Nebraska, Earth, and more than a little excited that my father was stationed at such an exotic—albeit peripheral—corner of the galaxy. I had no problem finding friends. They found me, alerted to my arrival by the rare appearance of a transport shuttle. After setting my suitcases down at Temporary Living Quarters, I opened my door in response to a knock, surprised to see not my parents, but another young teenager, shoulder-length brown hair and ice-blue eyes set among sharp features, smiling at me.

"Hi. I'm Robby, Robby Zewitt."

"Matt."

"So, you just got here, huh?"

"Yeah, freed from Nebraska, at last."

"Nebraska? Ouch!" Robby laughed. "Hey, doing anything?"

And from there our quick acquaintance took to friendship. Robby invited me to meet him at the "Zaal" after dinner. I would find it, he told me, about a mile up the river near permanent base housing—"can't miss it." Since all military bases are laid out essentially the same, I knew I would have no trouble finding it.

"Good hell, it's huge!" My voice sounded distant from my head, as if recorded then replayed from somewhere outside my own mouth.

"Wait till you get inside, Matt." Robby smiled that sort of smile that, though only acquainted for a few hours, made you simultaneously trust and wonder at him and his motives.

Jessica, Robby's thin, blonde girlfriend, did not share my unjaded faith in him. "No way. That place is haunted or something. Uh-uh. I'm not going in again. I'll wait out here. Actually, no—I'm going home. This place creeps me out." She walked off in the direction of her house. Robby blew her off with a wave of his hand.

The Zaal was quaint, I suppose. As quaint as an alien structure can be, anyway. Simple, yet beautiful. The earthly equivalent might be a giant pumice stone or some sort of coral—peach colored—riddled with man-sized holes, the inner walls of the tunnels ringed alternating blues and pinks like tropical octopus tentacles scooped of meat and turned inside out to penetrate the heights and depths of the immense rock. It floated—none of us knew how—about ten feet above the ground, an orange eye against the persistently gray, clouded sky. A clump of imported cork trees one hundred yards in diameter grew in its shadow—from these one might access the twelve-story high rock that had served—as I learned from my readings on the way from Delta Piscium—as a sort of monastery in ancient times, a sanctuary from the rest of the universe for those K'kli dedicated to reaching inward, to conquering themselves, their fears while the rest of their race reached outward to conquer their celestial neighborhood in a collective manifestation of those fears.

And it was rumored to be haunted. At least we Space Service brats agreed it was haunted. What other thrill could we claim as ours? We were denied the excitement of the more colorful bases—Black Shore 12, for instance, with its year-round seaside carnival, or Shifton Delta, the missile defense free-floating orbital platform, with its ski slope covered moon directly beneath, within an hour's transport time. No, Ixchill 7 was far from the center of the galaxy. But we had the Zaal. The Zaal set us apart. No one else had a haunted monument. Not even Earth, where most urban centers sat under Plexiglas domes filtering out and con-verting the carbon-dioxide drenched air into usable oxygen. The old Victorian mansions, the old castles had crumbled to dust well before the ecological disasters that drove man to live in the bubbles. The Zaal, then, was unique in all the known systems and, in our egocentric teenage human-ness, we felt it was ours, OURS, to explore.

Robby was first up the soft-barked trees. I was next, the new kid, the initiate. I was followed by Patti: red-haired tomboy and tough as nails— covered with scratches and freckles—and how she looked sexy to this puberty-stricken early teen. Reece, Robby's younger, more unsure brother, was last up.

Robby clambered into the closest hole and disappeared into phosphorescence-tinged darkness. I reached up and touched the sticky, rubbery surface and pulled myself in, crawling into the molten warmth of that pink and blue glow. Ahead of me, Robby's foot retreated through some kind of barrier, a valve, like a heart valve. I hesitated a half-second too long and Patti pushed me up through the plastic-textured film by my rear. A grin, a smirk, creased my face.

Gravity seemed to pull to the outside wall of the egg-shaped room no matter where one stood on the inside surface. I stepped aside—"up" was a valueless term in the Zaal—to let the other two through. Patti jumped out of the valve hole in her brusque manner, walking up to the "ceiling." Reece slowly poked his head through: "Ooh! We haven't been in here before!"

"Sssh!" the older brother chided. "Do you want to get caught?"

"The door was open—no big deal."

"Big deal if the security police find us in here," Patti smiled. "We're breaking and entering, Reece."

"Oh, yeah."

Robby slapped his forehead and shook his head. "Someone please tell me we're not of the same genetic makeup."

But by then the conversation had faded to background babble. I was caught up in the walls. They vaguely resembled a circuit board that had been shaped into a spheroid—lines leading to small circles leading to more lines to circles, ad infinitum. But these veins—pulsating with florescence, rainbow colors of light traveling along the conduit lines—seemed organic rather than mechanical. Not digital, but alive. The irregularity of patterning also added to the biological feel of the area—this was no room, it was...an organ.

We three boys watched the rainbow dance, spellbound, unwilling to tear ourselves from the sight until Patti called out to us. She knelt near another valve—I then noticed that the organ-room was full of them—and chided us:

"C'mon numb nuts! Here's a good one."

She disappeared "down" the hole. We followed, me in the rear now. We twisted and turned, writhing through the grooves of the alien brain, poking our heads through side branch valves into rooms vaguely similar to the first. I wondered, as we traveled, what tiny denizens might be lurking in my own gray matter. We moved swiftly through the tunnel, careful to keep our main throughway. One wrong trip down a side branch and it might take days to find our way out again—or be discovered by the security police or, worse yet, a K'kli diplomat visiting his ancestral haunts.

The K'kli were in temperament much like humans, more so than many of the non-Gaian races. They loved sociality, though they bore themselves aloof and detached when around humans, as if hiding some kind of adult secret from children. Their loyalty to one another and to tradition—including their deceased ancestors—was well known and well regarded by the human-friendly races. K'kli could be trusted to keep their word to a fault.

This knowledge came gradually, though, and those first human scouts who encountered the old race only grudgingly accepted their honesty. Their appearance did not help diplomatic matters. Their human-sized main trunk was egg-shaped and clear, their scintillating and ever changing rainbow-hued internal organs on view. One immense sucker at the bottom of the brilliant egg kept the body from tumbling over, especially when the cool, wet winds of Ixchill 7 blew through the three enormous spikes—eight feet in length or more, depending on the age of the creature—that surmounted the top of the body. Communication between members of the species takes place through color manipulation—another hindrance to early diplomatic efforts. Space Service intelligence officers took over three months, using the best in bio-computer technology, to crack the code. Even now, elements of their language are used in classified communications—or so the news media tells us.

I had seen K'kli from afar at the spaceport and was wondering how one would seem up close—How bright the colors? What did one smell like? Was their skin as rubbery and taut as these tunnel surfaces?—when Patti stopped, then plunged into a side passage. The others followed, driven by curiosity to see what could have possibly held Patti's flighty attention so firm.

The valve gave way and I stumbled through, bumping into Reece, knocking him to the floor in my eagerness to see just what had so intrigued Patti as to cause her to veer from our Ariadne's thread. Reece let out an "umph" but did not protest as I would have expected. His gaze was fixed upward, mesmerized. As I lifted my eyes from his sprawled form I too was struck by a quick shock, like a somnambulist suddenly awakening on the ledge of a skyscraper, traffic moving like flaming beetles below.

This chamber was different than the others, though the basic organic tone remained the same. The inner walls were laced circles interconnected with lines, but the pulsating color of other areas was absent. Here the synapses, as we thought of them, stood out in relief, as if carved from stone. Faint grayness glowed through the enormous room, giving a wan graveyard hue to the whole—a dead polyp off the main organ, abandoned to time and dust. And through the clouds of dust we saw protuberances from the chamber walls—small mounds of the gray stuff supporting the ashen corpses of hundreds, perhaps thousands, of desiccated and shriveled K'kli, their thorny crests poking towards each other from atop their mummified corpses, as if some impossibly gargantuan hedgehog had been turned inside out and we stood nestled in the forest of its spines. Fear mixed with equal doses of respect as we imbibed awe through our very skin. This was a place of reverence, we felt, a sacred chamber. I knew then that we had intruded where we ought not, seen a sight so staggering and esoteric that we might never hope to comprehend it all.

Patti broke the silence with a stuttering whisper, addressing the rest of us as we stood behind her: "I...I think we ought to go..." she turned, then stopped, gaze transfixed on something behind me—something immense. I turned in unison with Reece and Robby.

It was beautiful—and dreadfully large. I shook inside, waves of nervousness pulsed through my legs as I was flooded with hot flashes. My attention, my whole puny soul, focused on its throbbing essence of

Being Alive. Color coursed throughout its constantly shifting internal organs, chromatic fireflies in a lava lamp. The crest was tall—perhaps twelve feet above the body. No doubt this was a venerable elder. Orbiting the K'kli's head was a metallic insect-like voice transmission device, the same as those used by mutes back on Earth. The generic digitized voice warbled back and forth, in and out of hearing range as the miniature satellite circled the top of the organ sac. "I AM THE CURATOR...I Am The Curator...i am the curator...i am *** tor...i am the curator...I Am The Curator...I AM THE CURATOR..." The color-sound translator picked up speed as the elder approached us, spinning at a dizzying speed around the creature's head. "W-w-*-H-h-*-Y-y-* A-a-*-R-r-*-E-e-* Y-y-*-O-o-*-U-u-* H-h-*-E-e-*-R-r-*-E-e-*?" Finally, the aural disequilibrium faded as the device almost disappeared for speed, a choral streak of melded voices, a buzzing whir of electronica. "Why are you here? The Zaal is closed to visitors for the season."

Reece, poor, dumb Reece, stumbled on the perfect reply: "Uh, so when is it open?"

"Thursday through Saturday during the Summer months. You should have been briefed regarding this at school. Besides, your ignorance fails to justify your intrusion."

Robby instinctively came to his brother's aid: "One of your, uh, tubes was open. So we wandered in and...look, we're really sorry and we didn't know we weren't supposed to be in here," he lied.

"And what is your name, young human?"

"Steve, Steve Jones," he lied again.

We all followed suit, giving false names. I later learned that Steve Jones was Robby's high school nemesis. This was an intentional attempt to get the rival in trouble.

"You all know I will have to report this to the security police," the Curator chided.

Fugue XXIX

We mumbled our acknowledgement as a new fear coursed through us—what would happen when they found out (and they would find out) that we had all given false I.D.? Dad would come down on me like a thunderbolt—swift, sure and searing hot with anger. I committed myself to never trespass again.

The Curator led us, or rather herded us, through the intricate maze of tunnels—we were more lost than I had earlier supposed—and back to the original orifice through which we had gained entry. We climbed down the cork trees and fled, half-laughing, half gasping with jittery relief, to our homes where we expected our parents to be waiting, punishments prepared, upon learning of their delinquent teenagers activities.

They never did. The old K'kli didn't tell.

Only years later, as a government liaison to Ixchill 7 and its surrounding systems, did I understand the color-voice displayed by the Curator as it watched us descend from the Zaal:

"One thing is constant," it pinked to some unseen companion.

And it laughed—a roaring sky-blue laugh:

"Children are children."

Queen Phoebe

1. Foreground—a litter of mulling well-wishers, a county who's who of figureheads and politicatti come to congratulate the young groom and bride. Right—a sprawled mansion, immense, Romanesque, lacking the spires and spirals of the victors and Victorians down the road. A close-cut, gently sloping green hill rises left, behind and away from the boxy building and the group of celebrants on its lawn. At the hill's zenith a throne and atop the throne sits a small figure, child-like for size, but old, old, old with wrinkle and gray. A shining silver crown and unspotted white dress—plain, shining, flowing the length of the throne—lend an aura of purity to her decrepitude. A tuxedoed dwarf and a furry animal of some sort, possibly a cat, attend the royal figure, one on either throne side, as Queen Phoebe looks down on her serfs while they loiter on the estate's greens—*pigs wallowing in their mire.*

2. Lady Margaret Nesmith, the raven-haired hostess and executor of her crazed grandmother's estate, greets guests with a limp handshake and a quavering smile, revealing perfectly set teeth. Her nervousness is palpable. She hopes the brightly-colored tent awnings and loud music will distract the reception attendee's attention away from the white speck on the hill. The line has disintegrated by now and only the busiest of gossips gawk at the comely young bride, so Lady Nesmith sits at a table opposite her nephew's new wife. Black hair falls in cascades on the tablecloth as they lean over to speak with one another.

"Aunt Margie, thank you so much again for letting us hold the reception here."

"Oh, Sally, how could I deny my favorite nephew and his beautiful bride? How are you holding up with the crowds?"

"I'm well, though one does tire of embracing strange women reeking of perfume and shaking fat men's wet hands."

"Be grateful, young lady. Those fat men have fattened up your gift table."

"Uncharitable me. Please forgive. Have we got through all the relatives, then? Are there any I haven't met yet?"

"Only Grandmum. But, as you know, she's not fit to come down. It's best to leave her where she sits."

"Nonsense! I want to see all the relatives down here. She deserves a good time as much as the rest of us. I will invite her down myself if I must."

"She will not come, that I promise you. She's ill, Sally, both inside and out. I admire your sense of fairness, but leave it be."

"What does she do all day, then? Just sit there the year through? It's a wonder she doesn't die of cold with the wind blowing off the moor."

"Chiswick takes good care of her—he has since her youth. I am perpetually amazed that old fossil is still alive. The man must be pushing a century. Grandmum Phoebe does well with Chiswick. He holds an umbrella over her when it rains, wraps her in blankets when the cold comes, retrieves her food from the kitchen here at the mansion, attends to her every need. We never see her down here. She wants for nothing on the hill, why should she condescend to be with us in the old stone box?"

"Which reminds me—several of the guests think it a capital idea to hold the reception on the grounds, in the sun."

"No choice there, deary. Nesmith Hall is large, but the design is all wrong—it's a maze in there, worse than a jungle. A guest might be lost for days simply looking for the WC, especially the way this crowd is drinking."

"Well, Margie, I think I will go drink in some of the sights. After all, Benjamin and I have a long night ahead of us. I think I'll go recoup my energy—away from the crowds."

"Just don't wander too far! I'll keep my eyes on you."

The hostess is distracted by a tipped table. The bride enters a tent to ladle herself a drink from the punch bowl. No one sees her exit through a slit in the canvas and walk clumsily up the hill in her high heels.

3. *A petitioner.* Queen Phoebe motions to the herald, who presents her with the royal scepter. A hand rake changes hands, Chiswick bows before her highness. She sits up, proud, as her ancestors before her. There is a tradition to uphold, you see. Back from Phoebe to Henry to Henry to William to Solomon the temple builder, tradition—and poise. *Never let the petitioner sense your weariness or discomfort or sympathy. Any sign of weakness is a liability for, though you have been crowned by the grace and power of God, you are not invulnerable. Brutus's and traitors lie at every turn. You must strike first, before they remove you from your hard-won throne.*

Sally's gown billows like a snow drift as she reaches down to remove her ungainly shoes. Relieved of her hill-climbing hindrance, she throws back her veil and lifts the silken snow mound into her arms, continuing upward. The din of the crowd fades as she draws closer to the throne, the wind whistling in her ears, catching her dress as she approaches the peculiar trio.

What a beautiful lass, Queen Phoebe thinks.

"Good day, Mistress Nesmith, my lady."

Her dress is as white as my own.

"I thought I might invite you to join us below."

Her hair, so black.

"Would you care to come down for a moment?"

My hair was as dark when I wrested the throne from my predecessor so long ago, so long.

"You are free to bring your attendant and your pet too, if you wish."

You must strike before she removes you from your hard-won throne.

Chiswick cringes and cowers behind the throne, peeking his weasel-shaped greasy head out from under an arm as if anticipating doomsday. The young bride steps forward, kneeling down before the elderly figure-head, in deference to the queen. Only then does she notice that the cat is a husk, mummified skin clinging to the ribs of the disemboweled feline. Spiders crawl and weave webs through the body cavity, in and out of orifices, over matted fur. Queen Phoebe raises her scepter as the bride draws in a quick gasp.

4. Margie runs across the mansion grounds, pushing her way through the gape-mouthed crowd that watches as Sally descends the hill. The bride shuffles forward blindly, arms limp at her side, as twin fountains spout out from her empty eye sockets. She says nothing, breathing fast and hard, falling to her knees hyperventilating as crimson streams channel down over her breasts, soiling the white wedding gown with gore. An ambulance is called and a doctor administers aid as Lady Nesmith ascends the hill to the empty throne at its crest.

5. Grandmum and Chiswick are gone, as is the cat—how long had that lazy animal laid by the old woman's seat? It seemed like weeks. Well, it was gone now and Lady Nesmith has to find Grandmum before the authorities arrive—there will be inquiries. She walks up to the blood-spattered throne—clear evidence that the mad geriatric is indeed the culprit. A gleam of white flickers from the slope behind the throne and

Lady Nesmith bolts around the towering chair only to suddenly stop as if hitting an unseen wall.

White shines up at her in the dusk light, but not the white of Grandmum's dress as she had supposed. A pile of bones, basket-woven human ribs and femurs, tibia and scapulae inextricably entwined. Here a cloven skull, there a ruptured pelvic, human tooth marks on carpals and phalanges, a foramen magnum snapped at the edges—an impressionist's battlefield chalky with remains and calcified slivers and dust all pale and dry.

She turns to run back to the crowd and startles with a yelp at the suddenly-appearing gardener who reports his implements missing—hedge scissors, paring knife, hand rake, machete and a long-forgotten back door to the mansion swings open in the cool breeze somewhere near the orchard.

6. Several guests head inside the great hall, away from the excitement and the sirens and the gray moisture-laden sky as evening descends on Queen Phoebe's hill.

Headlong

Sergeant Drollop sipped his absinthe with a dainty pinky extended to the outside window, careful to keep his moustache dry of the green liquor.

"Surely, I shall win this time," he said to his companion across the carriage. She shifted in her seat, exposing enough thigh to cause Drollop's throat to tighten in anticipation of sweeter pleasures than racing. His opponents were not the only things that he would conquer this night, if he had his way.

The two could not have been dressed more differently: He in khaki colonial army dress, knee bandages drawn tight, riding crop and pith helmet on the seat beside him, his short cropped hair and tight wire moustache a testament to military crispness; she a blonde haired, blue eyed floozy complete with net stockings, feather boa and red corsetry. Her pouting ruby lips parted:

"The animals are well," she batted her eyelashes.

"Yes," Drollop gulped. "Prime physical specimens, these."

Outside, two gigantic gray lumps lurched ahead of the railroad carriage, tethered to it by thick rusted chains: taut, slack, taut, slack— the boxcar limped along the wrought iron highway. Two trenches plowed behind the pathetic creatures, dirt stained to ochre by the blood that seeped from the pachyderm's wounds.

"They have been trimmed, for aerodynamic efficiency," said Drollop, thumb pinched to forefinger as if punctuating the end of his phrase.

"And the driver?" she asked.

"One of our best."

The gas masked, white robed mahout sat sleeping atop the railcar, prodding lance lain across his lap, snoring in rhythm to the elephant pulls. Not even the loud snap and air whipping of the loosely stitched brown twine, used to suture the gaps where once were legs, trunks, ears, tails and eyes, awoke the weary driver. Only when the tusks stabbed the earth, jerking the car from off its tracks, did the jockey throttle out of the alpha state.

Drollop fell into the girl's lap, jarred from his seat by the sudden stop. She giggled and patted the absinthe from her breast with a hand-kerchief as the sergeant flew into a rage, kicking the carriage door open.

He brandished his kiboko, beating the driver with the rhinoceros hide whip.

"You imbecile! You careless moron! Now we are stranded, hours from Ngome, all because of what?"

The driver, crying, pointed to the Elephant-slugs. "They're broken."

Drollop ran to the closest animal, ripping the already loose tusk from its head, then set about pulverizing the driver's skull, the soft schlock, schlock of jelly mixed with bone signaling the coachman's final ride. He kicked the corpse, then, still enraged, stabbed the poor creatures' huge hearts with the tusk, their jittering convulsions causing the earth to shake under his feet.

"No. Now they are broken!"

Something immense fluttered in the trees.

Urizah had always failed. Since time began and before, something in his angelic genes assured a cock up at the most critical times. Or perhaps it was his human side. Giants always seemed destined for disappointment, ever since their winged fathers had raped the daughters of men in a bout of high cosmic testosterone. But Urizah was an exceptional failure—he excelled at bungling. Furthermore, he was far too large to mix with

197

humankind and his wings, molting and clumsy as they were, precluded him from the sociality of giants. Urizah didn't have many friends.

But now he would prove himself. He knew he had it in him. The cathedral bell-tower rang eleven, spurring him to flap harder, to accelerate to the glorious finish where he would glory in his success.

He crashed through the upper canopy, an explosion of flora heralding the breach. Blue blood, evidence of his biological inheritance from the Kingdom of Heaven, streaked his white robes, streaming in the wind, casting off tiny droplets of spray from the myriad cuts and scratches sustained on his journey thus far. The lacerations only served to stiffen his resolve. He pushed on through the moonlight, the forest a waving sea of chlorophyll beneath the leaf-rustling whump, whump of his enormous wings. He could see the cathedral on the horizon.

A thousand twig snaps and an explosion of black wings burst up from below—caw birds come to chase away the giant intruder. The beak cloud surrounded him, plucking his feathers, soiling his engraven halo with their waste—the TETRAGRAMMATON blasphemed. Several of the evil avian flock became entangled in his golden locks and in his eyes, his perfect blue eyes, like gems the size of melons, were pierced and popped to goo. He fell from the sky, ravens wedged in his every interstice, the purest white rictus clogged with black down and feathers. The crash resounded like a clap of thunder through the forest.

Something sluggish moved along the trail only a hundred feet from The Fallen One.

Queen Phoebe mushed the rickshaw driver, her dwarf servant Chiswick, along at a meager pace. His toil was minimal—the skinny old bat's age was a far larger number than her weight in pounds—but he made a show of it, panting forcefully as if the burden was almost too much to bear. A thin smile creased her wrinkled face—best that one's minion should know his proper place: suffering beneath his liege. Chiswick dearly hoped that his groveling would please her.

She could not win, and she knew it. Age had taken its toll on both she and her servant. One did not have to win, though, merely to finish. This parade was for the show. Her neighbors would sting with shame and envy for not having entered, for failing to garner the courage to compete. Her name would be spoken in reverent tones by the gossipists in their tea time sipping circles, a respectful hush falling over the group as she limped past. This was no race for Queen Phoebe: It was a political coup in which she would assume control over the social hierarchy of her caste, tiptoeing up the stepping stones of public embarrassment, shame, rumor and acclaim to bum rush the castle of respectability.

The rickshaw trundled on its rickety way.

Something bounded past the vehicle in the night.

Johnny Milkpodseed's spindly legs straddled his bouncy ball—a tightly sewn manatee skin bloated with stale air. Teeth jarred and eyeballs rolling, the freakish farmer guffawed in delight with each flat-footed size fourteen stomp of his cone-toed boots. Boredom drove Johnny on—harvest season was over, the crop of shrunken heads had been plucked from his purple orchard, even his faceless swine had birthed their deaf, dumb, blind, olfactory-deprived brood. There was nothing left to do but sit on the farmstead's hickory stool tinkering with projects, listening to the cool wet wind infiltrate the skeletal trees. But even his hobbies had lost their sweet savor—until he found his hobbyhorse.

Behind the boathouse, along the shore of the sterile, acidified lake, he found it. Insects skittered off in a cascade of antennae and dust as he pulled the gray parchment from beneath one of the rubbish middens that spotted the decrepit property. He spread out the morbid trophy along a pair of sawhorses looking, finding, the sphincter-valve and pumping the windbag full with his puny, mucous-soaked lungs. Five thousand and twelve puffs later, Johnny arose from his knees blue faced and wheezing and voila! Off to the races he went.

For hours, maybe geological epochs—Johnny's sense of time was nil—he boinged toward the echoing church bells, gleeful as a toddler girl with her new porcelain dolly. The tolling of the tower was the only thing keeping him on track. Several times he had been distracted from the goal—as if he had the capacity to give attention to anything other than his mechanical automasquirmers for more than a few minutes—but the bells pulled him back by the ear, like a puppeteer yanking on his stick-limbed brainless marionette.

But now another pull tugged at his black, shriveled heart strings, for there among the tree trunks, both hips scraping bark, waddled Olde Gwennyth Sedgewick. Fat Gwen, the hoo-hah boys called her. She heard the springing sound on the path and, spotting our hero, winked and wiggled her gargantuan rump at Johnny, beckoning him to the folds of her medieval rags. And so between the two of them, they licked the platter clean.

The manatee air bladder, left unattended, floated up to the leering moon.

Steady steps walked along the path.

The Child of Destiny had come.

And so the witching hour bell chimed as she walked aloof past the wreckage of the other pretenders. Here sat a giraffe-rider, his mount asprawl with a broken neck, there a parachutist constricted by a tangler tree, further a dark autochthon being chased by a giant cat—the fanged beast bent on retrieving its dermis. Through all the ruckus The Child of Destiny walked calm, black hair flailing in the rising gale as she shoved open the cathedral's biolithic double doors.

There the contest's previous champions awaited in a moment of silence as the doors swung apart. Then joy and rejoicing! The rapture of the win as their screams echoed off the clerestory, bright beings of light ululating for their new comrade, and she takes her seat at the gold throne in the apse, the heroine of the race, ready to receive her reward.

She was crowned with a laurel wreath and, like every winner before her, smiled and waved to the ectoplasmic, glowing crowd as the hooded executioner brought down the stone sledge on her head, smashing the bregma into encephalonic jelly. Her reward: Apotheosis.

And as the last ting of the bell faded into night, her body sat alone, crowned and enthroned in the cold stone darkness of the abandoned cathedral. The other contestants parted ways, leaving the desolate wilderness, for no sane being would remain in that place for long and there was no more prize to be won: The Child of Destiny had broken the ribbon, taken the key, passed to the winner's circle to become one with the haunting hosts of previous victors. And the cathedral, save for the faint drip of blood, remained silent.

The Further Adventures of Star Boy

Star Boy's tale begins with an ending, as transgressive stories often do. He lay in a trash can, dying. Refuse, in turn, lay on him like layers of spuria and outright lies: egg shells, green molded orange peels, spent condoms, and the business page of your local paper, replete with headlines only you would understand due to your own unique life experiences. Your life. Not the life of Star Boy. But this is his tale. Not yours. No.

The life of Star Boy was conceived in disorder, a stochastic and grand cosmic mistake. But, despite the chaos, one can recount the series of mishaps that led to his pathetic existence in an orderly manner, like peeling off the waste that covered him as he lay dying in that filthy steel drum. It began with the unfortunate confluence of several not-necessarily-opposed pairs: stupidity and luck, music and drugs, ignorance and lust, selfishness and lack of self-esteem, penis and vagina, sperm and egg. All, of course, manifested through Star Boy's mother and father and their not-necessarily-opposed procreative organs.

Of his father we shall speak little, for he contributed not more than one sperm cell to the entirety of this story (and a faulty one, at that). Yes, you might argue that the data-encrusted tapeworms of DNA coding found within that sole albino eel are critical to the formation of Star Boy and, hence, to our understanding of him as a self-sentient being. But I defy you to unravel the hermitic mystery of which specific characteristics he inherited from his mother and which from his father. Such esoterica is likely hidden from you, if I judge correctly. Besides, this is his tale, not yours. Consider carefully the hubris of assigning your judgments to his story.

Of his mother we might say some few things, as she, unlike his good-for-nothing father, was present for, and contributed much to Star Boy's entry into our bountiful blue world. She housed him, as it were, while he developed and subsequently emerged from the churning swill of recessive genes, syphilis, psychoactive drugs, and vodka that flooded her womb. And she bore him, a laborious task of white-hot pain, were it not for the cocktail of drugs that she consumed before transition began. The doctors and nurses need not have medicated her, as her self-medication was more than sufficient. But they did, pumping her full of dulling syrups and narcotics, which might explain Star Boy's recollection of her as a woman of beauty under a head of luxurious red hair, full of motherly kindness, soft, gentle, loving. After all, the placenta can't be expected to filter every foul substance, especially a placenta marinated in alcohol and a mind-numbing array of drugs, as was his mother's. It was inevitable that some loose hallucinogens should get through and addle the boy's mind and warp his vision.

They did.

She was anything but beautiful, and her only kindness was manifested in not killing the child outright, fresh off the stirrups. One part of his memory is correct, though—she did have long, curly red hair. Beneath that red wire mop slumped an almost-expressionless face, devoid of emotion save when some mind-altering pharmaceutical pulled the immense jowls up into an artificial smile—a wooden marionette's grin, clearly controlled by some master other than its owner. He mistook the glistening perspiration that covered her face and body for a heavenly glow and, misjudging her drugged smile as a sign of approving condescension, thought of her as an angel gently lowering him into the river of temporal existence from some veiled pre-life, trailing clouds of glory.

Had he the capacity to understand earthly languages, he might have been able to discern his true position vis-à-vis his mother, except that experience had not yet taught him a tongue other than that of the angels. Experience also had not, indeed could not have, yet taught him the principles of sarcasm and rejection that we adults understand so readily.

"Agh, my aching crotch."

"Miss Wittgenstein, it's a boy!"

"Crotch hurts. More drugs."

"Miss Wittgenstein, your baby, it's a boy!"

"Hunh? Oh, nice. Gotta sleep."

"Oh, but we've got to get that placenta moving out. You're not quite done yet. Miss Wittgenstein? Ma'am, you'll need to wake up. Ma'am? Nurse!"

It was all as the sound of golden trumpets and angelic choirs to Star Boy's malformed ears. Had he been able to understand another conversation, mere hours after the first, the intervening time spent being spanked, stuck with needles, and washed with cold cloths—all an exercise in training him that only mother could really nurture him, really comfort him—perhaps, if he had the ability to interpret this dialogue, he might have understood the gravity of his life's situation and possibly even seen through the darkened mists of un-spent time to the future that awaited him in eternal anticipation, but was never satisfied by his arrival. Blissful ignorance enshrouded him, though, the words caressing his cochlea with warmth and false reassurances.

"Miss Wittgenstein, I'd like to speak openly with you about your son."

"Your prerogative."

"Your son has a condition known as *Corpus Astralis*. It's a rather rare developmental issue in which the fingers and toes do not fully develop. As a result of, er, the introduction of foreign substances into the fetus, the arms and legs of those with the condition do not grow as most babies do. You'll find that the limbs are much thicker at their connection with the torso than at the ends. This is also true of the place on the body where the neck meets the spine. The skull is elongated and is likely to retain its conical shape, as will the boy's limbs. He is not likely to grow much larger than his present size, Miss Wittgenstein. As a result of this 'astral syndrome,' as it is sometimes called, you'll have to take special care of the boy. Resources are available for you to help you in what will likely be a demanding process of raising the boy."

"Raising the boy? Oh, yeah. I'll take care of him. Of that."

"Good. Then before we release the two of you, we'll need you to decide on your son's name for the records."

"Name. Let's see. Last night, for the first time, I clearly saw the universe in all its splendor. Galaxies raced past me in my wake while planets whirled round and round on a cosmic carousel. For this reason I will name the boy Star. Star Wittgenstein."

Thus began the very short legal existence of the entity known to us as Star Boy. Of course, the boy existed physically before being named, possessing a personality (John Locke burn in hell with his *tabula rasa*), likes and dislikes, even infantile desires. Don't take me for a jaw-gaped idiot. But names are a matter of states and governments, and who are you question the behemoth that is political structure, you who are so small, merely a number on an identification card under the panoptic gaze of an immense gun-wielding bureaucracy?

The name lasted not an hour. Star Wittgenstein, legal entity, was unceremoniously dumped into a trash can at the side of the hospital by his mother. She then ran (well, hobbled quickly, really, given her condition) into the street, screaming for "a hit of crack" before being struck by a south-bound semi-truck pulling a 53' trailer full of frozen chicken. She was struck cold and dead as the poultry therein, though at a much higher velocity. And with her life and the accidental loss of certain files—due to an act of fornication in the records department—went the memory of Star Wittgenstein, legal entity. And this is where the beginning ends and the end begins.

As the child lay dying in fever dreams of mother, a bright light shone beyond, at the terminus of a tunnel. And at the end of that tunnel a presence, a warm presence, arms reaching out to enfold the child. It was not God, but the head master of a local orphanage, shining his flashlight down into the trashcan, into Star Wittgenstein's—correction: into Star Boy's—blue eyes in an effort to ascertain whether the child was alive or dead. Still, the mescaline/shroom/LSD concoction fed to him through his mother had not yet worn off, so Star Boy felt assured that God had come to gently remove him from the river of temporal existence into some veiled post-life, the dust of Adam's transgression sloughing from him like so much meconium.

To the orphanage went Star Boy, wrapped in burlap and hamburger wrappers, swaddled against the cold night by rough cloth and grease, a paper-thin layer of insulating fat. This proved beneficial, as the tall, gaunt frame of Headmaster Thumbswallow did little to stop the wind-whipped rain that had begun pattering down on the pair as they traversed and transected the city by way of alley, overpass, backyard, and storm water drain-off pipes until, finally, they arrived at the antiseptically-named, yet un-antiseptically filthy, *God's School for Wayward Youth*. Star Boy's inability to read saved his sanity, for if the child had somehow learnt literacy before the drugs wore off, he surely would have fallen to the ground in uncontrolled convulsions of religious ecstasy and been forever locked with one foot in heaven, as he supposed it, and one on earth. He did fall into convulsions, but this was the result of a latent epilepsy, rather than a rhapsodic awakening.

The orphanage itself was rather like its inhabitants. It was cold and made of stone, much like the hearts of those who lived and worked there. It was in obvious disrepair and decay, like the lives of all therein. And the building seemed to throw itself on Star Boy, to reach a bit beyond the bounds of its inanimate frame to strike the child with brick corners and solid oak doors as he thrashed upon the doorstep, much as the boys (for either there were no wayward girls or God did not want them at his school) would throw themselves on him in ways that assured him that those who lived here were, indeed, wayward in the eyes of God.

I will spare you the tedious recounting of the many years of daily beatings administered to Star Boy by headmaster and fellow student alike. For what could you know of such suffering from the comfort of your armchair in your heated house? You are clearly incapable of even imagining the shame administered to him at the hands, feet, and other appendages of those in God's school. Can you comprehend the humiliation, so long after his introduction to the school, after burning away the best years of his innocence, of being told you are going to go on a field trip, only to be thrashed in the street and left unconscious in the burning-cold confines of a trash can? Star Boy can. Is it even possible for you to bring to mind the smells and textures of squalor and the helpless inability to escape that which is thrust upon your senses? It is for Star Boy. And can you imagine the joy of being rescued from such circumstances, the red flash of ambulance lights breaking like a new dawn over the lip of your prison-can? Can you? Star Boy can imagine, and vaguely remembers that moment through a half-delirious haze not unlike those of his drugged infancy.

Fugue XXIX

In his newly-blossomed adolescence, though, Star Boy was wiser, yet not crafty, more experienced, but not yet jaded, aware, yet still possessing that bright hope that had sustained him thus far—the vision of his red-haired Madonna and her flowing halo. That brightness was kindled in the emergency lights as he was driven to the hospital—*that hospital*, where his life had begun and his mother's so abruptly ended, the very cradle of his civilization, his Sumer, his Alexandria. The delivery doctor had, unfortunately, since retired and moved to Malibu. And so the means of his mother's demise must remain, to him, a mystery forevermore.

A new doctor was assigned his strange case, a doctor more suited to performing abortions than saving patients whom most would think ought to have been aborted long ago. Nevertheless, is this not the nature of bureaucracy, to assign the unassigned where they ought not to be? The un-aborted, but barely viable, to the one man capable of finishing this tale before it ever started, had the channels of fate seen fit? The named to the nameless? Of course, you can't be expected to answer such questions.

This doctor had a name, Doctor Leonard, though the mute Star Boy was unable to pronounce the name. The portion of the boy's brain that facilitated speech was at the farthest possible point from his speech-making organs, at the apex of his stellar body. Another organizational debacle. This distance between synapses also prevented protestation when Star Boy realized that the doctor, finding no legal evidence of the boy's existence, was doctoring records in order to fake the injured boy's death. The portion of his brain that controlled reason, though, was only a short distance from his heart—the seat of emotion—thus he was able to comprehend, with an attendant foreboding, that the doctor's actions were clearly in breach of the Hippocratic Oath.

His heart sank (away from reason) as the doctor wrapped him in bandages—many more bandages than his wounds justified—and gently lowered him into a trash can out back. This time, Star Boy could not tell whether he was being submerged or retrieved from any kind of river into any kind of life, mortal or post-mortal. This lack of surety caused him great fear.

He waited for the dread light in the tunnel. But before Headmaster Thumbswallow could retrieve him on his nightly rounds through the back streets of the city, Doctor Leonard retrieved the child from the bin and drove him far, far across town, farther than he had ever traveled before. Star Boy watched from the Volvo's heated leather passenger seat as they twisted and turned in an upward-spiraling swirl of increasingly-affluent neighborhoods, mansions stacked on condos stacked on mansions, up to the best views of the valley below. It was as if he were traveling up through the clouds to take his place in the heavens. The doctor said something about Marx and tax cuts and laughed, but Star Boy was too mesmerized by the glitter of lights to pay much attention to him until they pulled into a parking garage underneath a hill crest condominium that the orphanage boys would have described as "swank."

Doctor Leonard carried Star Boy up swank stairs, into a swank elevator, down a swank hallway, and through a swank set of double doors, behind which was what could have been a very swank condo, save for the décor. True, bronze nude mermaid statues, the jet black electronics, and mural-sized modern art canvases, composed mainly of swaths of color in varying shades of blue, simply reeked of swank. But interspersed among the green marble pillars of the main living room were stacks of aquariums, all filled with formaldehyde in which floated a golden array of misshapen bodies, an eerily-preserved carnival sideshow of conjoined twins, undeveloped fetuses, hermaphrodites, and club-foot malformities. All these were lit from underneath scattering yellowed shimmers, like undulating liquid amber, across the blue walls of the room. Ambient music played from speakers in the ceiling, increasing the dream-like atmosphere of that bizarre trophy room.

For a moment, Star Boy startled from his ease as the thought entered his conical brain that perhaps Doctor Leonard meant to pickle him, like the rest of his genetically-inferior mates behind the glass. But the good doctor sensed this trepidation and placed a reassuring hand on his sharply-angled shoulder. Star Boy knew, in that moment, that however strange the doctor's motives, he did not mean to harm the young man. Further reassurance was now walking through the door from an adjacent bedroom.

From the doorway at the end of the aquarium columns exploded a rush of red light that cast a warm glow over the living room, turning the shimmering yellow waves into an orange fire that consumed the room, as if in flame. In that doorway stood a curvaceous silhouette: tall, slender, and long-legged. Only when the woman entered the room could he see her clearly, albeit bathed in a crimson glow. Her auburn hair cascaded down to the curve of her hip, sensual eyes cut the air with their green intensity. Her round, puffy lips contrasted with the sharp angularity of her face, giving her the appearance of the everlasting pout that men find so inebriatingly passionate. She wore a dark green dress tight enough that Star Boy wondered how it was ever put on in the first place. Beneath the ankles of the dress, at the bottom of the slit that rose well up her smooth thigh, was a pair of thinly-strapped high-heeled shoes fastened firmly to her slender feet.

She looked at Doctor Leonard with what might have been an expression of disapproval. But the doctor did not seem to take it so. He smiled at her and nodded his head, looking from her to Star Boy. She slowly turned her face in the direction of Star Boy, not moving her eyes from the doctor's face until the last possible moment, when her eyes flicked over to him like an adder's strike, locking on his eyes. She smiled, seeming to like what she saw in his eyes, then scanned over his body with an intensity that made him inexplicably uncomfortable. The discomfort left him, though, as flashbacks of his mother projected themselves onto his waking vision, superimposing a partially-opaque image of her onto this beautiful woman. Gradually, the image of his mother's face faded and he realized, to his hurt, the true extent of his mother's ugliness. Yet he was comforted as this woman's face filled him with admiration for her beauty, with a need to be accepted by her, and, for the first time in his life, the unfamiliar, yet quickly rising tide of pure lust. The intensity of his need throbbed like a beating heart in his ears, and it was only with difficulty that he heard the woman's conversation with the doctor.

"He," she hesitated, visibly trembling. "He is...beautiful."

She caressed Star Boy's head and limbs as the doctor spoke in a low growling voice seething with anticipation.

"I knew you would like him. He is a gift."

"For me?" She placed one hand over her chest in delight. Star Boy wished she would put her hand back on him.

"For us," Doctor Leonard's eyes sparkled.

"For us, yes," she said, standing and letting the dress slink impossibly to the floor. She wore only her smooth, pale skin beneath.

And there, in the light of fire, was Star Boy introduced to the musings of the flesh by Doctor Leonard and his mistress, an interlocked trio of bodies surrounded by a museum of physical imperfections, perfectly preserved.

The woman, named Marquette—he never did learn her last name—was an art dealer who owned the swankest of galleries in the downtown. She was never unkind to Star Boy, even when she took him to various and sundry opening shows with a leather leash in her hand, the other end lovingly clasped around his "neck" above the tuxedo he habitually wore on important nights out. Indeed, he might easily have removed the cylindrical top hat from his dunce cap head and slipped the leash from his neck, but he felt no need. For when they were alone, or together with Doctor Leonard, or participating in the lushness of group "activities" (conical limbs and head were ideal for such situations—he was, indeed, the center of much attention), he knew that he was more than a mere object of sexual gratification. A tenderness informed her every word and touch. Outside of the bedroom, on days and nights when Marquette was not needed at the art gallery (or when the showiness of it all bored her), they enjoyed carriage rides through the country, ferris wheel rides at the fair, and gondola rides on the river. Indeed, they could hardly keep still. For years they moved in restless circumlocomotions and spiraling ambulations, like a binary system slowly spinning around an immense black hole.

The chances of their being home on that fateful October night, then, were almost astronomical. They had been out looking at fall colors all day, enjoying the blaze of autumn, and were just stripping down with Doctor Leonard for a night of bodily exploration when the front doors of the condominium crashed open. One of the doors fell from its top hinge to hang awkwardly from the bottom hinge, like a half-picked scab at an odd angle, into the front foyer. Through the breach rushed a half-dozen goons in three-piece suits one size too small for their thickly-muscled bodies. From the back of the group emerged a short, paunchy man of dark complexion and dark stares whose eyes flicked from side to side, as if he were espying clues in order to solve some esoteric mystery or find some hidden lurker.

Star Boy looked on in naked terror—for he had successfully extricated himself from his clothes before the unlikely intrusion. Doctor Leonard was still half-dressed, though, as he approached the group, the doctor's confidence drained out of him through a growing wet spot on his pants. His face had gone as pale as his monogrammed, button-up shirt.

"Ah, Angelo," his voice shook with a magnitude of about 7.8, though his volume was almost undetectable.

"Doctor Leonard. The bills have come due," he said without humor.

"Ah, Angelo. I'm, ah, prepared to pay you tomorrow." The wet spot grew and carved a river down his leg.

"But Doctor Leonard. The credit check is over. Your invoice is past due. Time to pay interest."

"Ah, Angelo!" the doctor screamed as the goon squad wrapped duct tape around his mouth, wrists, arms, ankles, and legs to the sobbing of Marquette. The ambient music from the speakers took on a sinister tone as a pair of goons thrust the doctor head-first into one of the largest aquariums, holding him by his ankles under the stinging formaldehyde, face to genitalia with the wrinkled hermaphrodite's sexes. In time the convulsions subsided. Marquette was similarly introduced as the newest member of her museum, though she was too stunned to scream and, thus, did not require duct tape over her fulsome lips. Star Boy wondered at the restraint practiced by Angelo and his goons in *not* raping her and murdering her, but in merely murdering her. He was ashamed to feel admiration for them in this regard.

Fear flushed to the top of his pointed head as Marquette slowly sank, lungs full of preservative, into a tank previously filled with a dozen fetuses, like seahorses bobbing up and down on the formaldehyde tide. They circled her form, and Star Boy wondered if it was the action of her body being put into the liquid that caused their motion, or if they had somehow sapped the last of her dying energy and gleefully spun around to mock her with their newfound life force.

The goons turned to him, advancing with purpose. He could do naught but sit naked and await his doom. He wondered into which gallery his strange body would be displayed. None of the tanks looked very inviting, to say the least.

But Angelo, in his magnanimity, held up a restraining hand.

"The baby comes with me. Wrap him up in blankets. Gently."

The "baby"—though eighteen years of age by the time of his capture—was raised by the DiAmalfo family, Angelo's godfather's second-cousin's wife's uncle's family, to be exact. The DiAmalfo's were continually amazed at the child's ability to learn so quickly, walking within mere days (his legs shook for almost a week after witnessing Leonard and Marquette's murders), potty training in mere weeks (*ibid* for his bowels and bladder, only they took longer to bring under control), and able to understand grown-up talk in mere months (this was not a side-effect of fear, but an act of willful ignorance while he feigned incomprehension in order to have time to observe and get his bearings in the strange and dangerous culture of the *Cosa Nostra*). As a perceived infant, Star Boy was able to infiltrate the most secret of chambers without consequence ("Oh, look Rudolfo, there's the baby. Now would you please put him back in the nursery while I kill Antonio here for botching the Indiglio job? Thanks. Bye-bye, baby, we wuv woo!")

So when the boy came of age at twenty-one (38, to be more precise), it was no wonder that he rose quickly through the ranks of the family as the most intelligent and respected and ruthless of its members. He was admired for his silence, though only he knew that its maintenance depended not on discipline, but on the shape of his brain. He was thought by others to be a genius, studying, as he did, medical texts late into the night to gain an understanding of they knew not what. And they never laughed at him. Ever.

But they could not know, nor could you know, save I reveal it to you, the inner turmoil that wracked his soul. For his enforced silence was anathema to him, and his studies were only the symptoms of craving in a hopeless search to understand and cure his incomprehensible and un- curable condition. He wished to be able to speak, to be truly loved, to express love and beauty through word, voice, and song. But with a mouth that would not speak and hands that would not type, he could only be understood in the most general of terms by his underlings and those around him. Thankfully the dullards understood enough to take care of the family business that he needed done.

It was while wrapped in the arms of depression that he sought out those two things (well, two of the many things) that simultaneously comforted and killed his mother: drugs and sex. He skipped marijuana and hallucinogens, bypassed methamphetamines, and scoffed at cocaine in all its forms as he drove straightway into an intravenously- administered heroin addiction. It was difficult to find good veins on his arms, so he immediately went for injections to the neck.

Likewise, he skipped the finer points of sex, eschewing pornography, belittling extra-marital affairs, even foregoing the delights of sexual experimentation with other men, animals, and children, and scoured the underworld for the most despicable, ugly, diseased and cranky of trans- vestite prostitutes. He flew from city to city, at great expense, to revel in the dilapidated wastelands of their creaking, bug-infested beds. Of course you recoil in disgust, but what can you know of Star Boy's desires and the satisfaction he derived therefrom? Judge not. You know nothing.

The expenses became so high between his heroin use and leer-jet rendezvous with debauchery, in fact (there is a wonderfully filthy broth- el on the outskirts of Ulaanbaatar, for instance, that he frequented quite often, but only after a visit to The Cherry Farm in rural Nevada), that Angelo's debt collectors had to visit him, on business, of course, one night in South Chicago.

Fugue XXIX

There was nothing elegant about this visit. Here, a sparseness of prose is called for to illustrate his thoughts:

A whore.

A door.

A goon.

A gun.

A run.

A fall.

A window.

A crash.

A longer fall.

A hard landing.

A crack of bones.

Dead whore underneath.

A bleeding conical head.

A gnarled hand emerging from under a pile of trash.

Blackness.

Dreams.

Hamlet's mill, the prow of Poseidon's craft thrusting up from the sea and into the stars, carving twin whirlpools above and below, water indistinguishable from void, vortexing points of light smeared into glowing pinwheels against inky indigo darkness, then into one rotating nuclear furnace blob of star aging blue, green, yellow, orange, red, expanding until it floods the whole of Star Boy's field of vision, consuming his eyes.

And he awakes with no recollection of anything whatsoever. A new birth. Held in the arms of an old, haggardly bag lady who coddles him as they lay in a trash bin, she trying to force her "dolly's" misshapen head onto a wrinkled tit. And he drinks and suckles and the heartbeat of the old crone slows and dies as the bin is lifted into the air and the contents spill into a dump truck, sending him tumbling under a mountain of trash. The truck vibrates, squeaks, and drives out into the country towards whatever place South Chicago waste goes.

He peels away the trash, layer by layer, ascending through the morass of waste, unsure of where he is, who he is, why he is here. A newspaper flutters above him, but he has forgotten how to read. It then flies awkwardly away, like a bat, into the night and he looks up into the rural sky, unhindered by city lights and sees that glowing band splayed out across the darkness. And he begins to remember the inkling of a name.

Star Boy's tale ends with a beginning, as transgressive stories often don't.

About the Author

Forrest Aguirre recently received the World Fantasy Award for his editorial work on *Leviathan 3*. He was also a finalist for the Philip K. Dick Award for this work. His own fiction has appeared in a variety of well-respected publications including *Notre Dame Review* and *Prague Literary Review*.

He recently edited *Leviathan 4* and is finishing work on his first novel, *Swans Over the Moon*. He has also begun editing a new anthology series, *Text:Ur*, the first volume of which will be entitled *The New Book of Masks*. Forrest lives in Madison, Wisconsin with his wife and four children.

Coming in 2006
from Raw Dog Screaming Press

Text:Ur vol. 1
The New Book of Masks

Fantastical fiction from the most imaginative minds
of our time. A beautifully surreal masquerade fea-
turing fiction by Rikki Ducornet, Lance Olsen, Tamar
Yellin, and many others. A hallucinogenic spectacle
of literary experimentalism, brought to you by World
Fantasy Award winning editor Forrest Aguirre.

For more info visit
www.rawdogscreaming.com

Pseudo-City
D. Harlan Wilson, 128 pgs

www.rawdogscreaming.com

In Pseudofoliculitis City nothing is as it seems and everything is as it should be. Today's forecast calls for extreme confrontation, with sandwich flurries and the threat of handlebar mustaches to the west.. By turns absurd and surreal, dark and challenging, Pseudo-City exposes what waits in the bathroom stall, under the manhole cover and in the corporate boardroom, all in a way that can only be described as mind-bogglingly irreal endings.

Westermead by Scott Thomas, 292 pgs

Ways of old merge with the magical in this wondrous world. Experience Westermead's thaw and awakening season by season, the lush heat of summer's passion and the retreat into winter's desolate embrace. Come celebrate and mourn with the people of Westermead as they make their way through a world steeped in beauty and dread. With storytelling this vibrant, it's easy to get lost in Thomas' unique landscape.

Tempting Disaster editor John Edward Lawson, 260 pgs

An anthology from the fringe that examines our culture's obsession with sexual taboos. Postmodernists and surrealists band together with renegade horror and sci-fi authors to re-envision what is "erotic" and what is "acceptable." By turns humorous and horrific, shocking and alluring, the authors dissect those impulses we deny in our daily lives. Includes stories by Carlton Mellick III, Michael Hemmingson, Lance Olsen & Jeffrey Thomas.

Play Dead by Michael A. Arnzen, 272 pgs

Johnny had given up cards for good until he stumbled onto a different game. A game where you have to make the cards before you play them and the stakes are the highest he's ever seen. When the payout is survival and folding means death the question becomes: are you playing the cards or are they playing you? Using 52 chapters Arnzen's novel-of-cards is stacked with mischief and thrills. Like the most accomplished blackjack dealer Arnzen will keep you guessing at his hand.

www.ingramcontent.com/pod-product-compliance
Lightning Source LLC
Chambersburg PA
CBHW050523260626
47157CB00004B/1451